DISTANT
JOURNEYS

DISTANT JOURNEYS

An Illustrated Anthology of Fantasy & Science Fiction

Edited by James B. King

ISBN 0-9627030-6-0

Library of Congress Catalog Card Number 96-68749

Printed in U.S.A.

Sovereign Seal Books are published by StarLance Publications, 5104 Cooperstown Lane, Pasco Washington 99301

Contents

Preface *by James B. King*   7

Rage and Fury *by Selina Rosen*   8

The Spheres of Acamar *by Richard N. Dunbar, Sr.*   16

The Hunter *by Gerard Daniel Houarner*   25

The Cyborg Touch *by A. J. Sobczak*   35

When the Sun Makes Darkface *by Mary E. Choo*   45

Aisha Kydyshia *by David Niall Wilson*   55

A Story from the War *by M. Shayne Bell*   62

Not Another Unicorn *by Mary Soon Lee*   71

Biological Imperative *by John Everson*   79

Unnatural Balances *by Jim Lee*   89

The People of the Wind and Sand *by B. J. Thrower*   96

The Domain was Fire. The Laws. *by Thomas Canfield*   110

The Authentic Article *by Diane de Avalle-Arce*   118

Thrill *by Will Greenway*   125

Illustrators

Scott A. Becker   16, 55, 62, 96

Donald W. Schank   34, 44, 78, 88, 118

Richard A. Tomasic   8, 24, 70, 110, 124

Cover illustration by Gary A. Kalin

Preface

I can still recall, as a youth, my first journeys into the realms of fantasy and science fiction, first through worn and well-read editions of Edgar Rice Burroughs' *John Carter of Mars* series and then Burroughs' *Tarzan* series, given to me by or borrowed from friends and relatives. I was seduced by these awe-inspiring, fascinating adventures; I had been snared.

I soon discovered the science fiction section in the closest bookstore and–what luck!–had barely enough money to buy my first science fiction novel, C. J. Cherryh's *Brothers of Earth*, purchased more because it was a small book and was less expensive than others on the shelves. I was unaware that Cherryh was a relative newcomer to the field. Not that it would have mattered. I was enthralled; what a wonderful story! A thirteen-year-old could not ask for a greater adventure. In the months following I purchased every Cherryh novel I could find and soon discovered other authors as well.

When fans of the genre talk about the author or authors who inspired their devotion to science fiction, they usually mention names like Poul Anderson, Philip Jose Farmer, L. Sprague de Camp, Robert A. Heinlein, Arthur C. Clarke, and Isaac Asimov. I discovered the works of these authors only later. But all have taken me on great and wonderful journeys, some to far off places, some not so distant. But, when I have to answer the question, "What is your favorite book?" my mind goes back to the first novel that I had purchased with my own money and added to my very small library to be read again and again, and I must answer, *"Brothers of Earth."* It was truly my first, very own distant journey.

May we all cherish our own special distant journey, may there be no end to our adventures into strange and fantastic worlds, and may you find as much pleasure in reading the journeys presented here as I did in preparing them for you.

– James B. King

Rage and Fury
by Selina Rosen

Hate could devour you. Shana knew that. She just didn't care anymore.

Anger was a cruel task master. But it din't ask for much warmth.

Bitterness was easy. It crept into your soul, like a secret lover crept into your bed and clung to you till you lost yourself.

She sat in the corner of the tavern

alone and far removed from the two men she had worked with for over six years. There were two reasons for this, actually. This first being that it was safer this way. The second was that she preferred it this way.

It hadn't always been like this. She watched them as they laughed and drank across the room and the bitterness washed over her like a black wave as she thought of the relationship she had once had with them. It was lost forever now. Like everything else.

She checked the cloth that covered her face and hid her shame.

There was a young—not very talented—bard playing a tune on a lute in the corner. The music wafted through the other tavern sounds and by the time it reached Shana's ears, it was barely recognizable. But it was a happy tune, so Shana hated it.

Out of the corner of her eye, she saw a stranger approach her friends. She grasped the hilt of her sword, which leaned unsheathed against her leg. She would have done that in any case, but something about this fellow made her uneasy. Something about him stirred things in her that she wished left alone.

CONNER AND Gareth sat at the bar, sharing conversation and beer. Conner was a young man with boyish good looks. His hair and well-kept beard were reddish-blond and his blue eyes sparkled with mischief. He wasn't a big man. Of moderate height and build, he looked like a smith or a farmer, anything but a merc. Gareth was a complete contrast. There was no doubt what Gareth was. The older mercenary wore the scars of his trade. His brown hair and brown beard had been allowed

to go their way long ago. His brown eyes looked troubled and wary. He was a little taller than Conner and a little heavier—especially in his gut.

"Where did she go?" Conner asked.

"Back booth, right corner," Gareth answered. Conner nodded.

"Our friend, the perpetual paranoid," Conner said, shaking his head. "She would find disease in the milk of human kindness."

Gareth laughed. "Aye and that attitude has saved us all on more than one occasion."

"Yes. Well, I miss the old days, when she would sit at the bar with us and share our beer and a story or two." Conner said with a bitterness all his own. "I miss Shana. The Shana we used to know. This *thing* doesn't even *resemble* her."

"I'll hear no more of that, Conner." Gareth scolded. "For all Shana has been through, she has coped well. Better than you or I would have. Let us not forget all that she has lost. She *has* changed. I'll not argue with you over that. But I still believe that somewhere under it all, our friend is still intact and someday she will indeed come back to us."

Conner didn't agree. He nodded, took a sip of beer and pretended that all was well in the world. That Shana was exactly the same as she had been before the world had crumbled and they had all been ruined. He wished sometimes that he could be as blind as Gareth, but he couldn't. Work had been hard to come by since the disaster at Talgar. They'd had to keep dipping into their surplus money till there was none. Over the last year, they had hocked everything but the bare essentials.

Conner wanted to stay with Shana and Gareth. He had worked with them for almost five years. They were the closest thing to a family that he'd ever had. But Conner was young; his best years as a merc were yet to come. Being with a poor, dwindling troop wasn't helping him make a name for himself.

They had been a respected and wealthy group, twelve members strong. But the ones who hadn't died at Talgar had left in the lean times that followed.

Conner knew he'd have to go soon, if he was to have any future. Gareth was getting too old to convince people that he was a serious merc––though Conner knew that Gareth was more than capable of taking on men half his age and twice his size. Shana men knew by deed and her skill no one would question. But no one wanted to hire her. They knew her mind was not all there and they didn't trust her. To be blunt, they knew she should be dead. The fact that she was still breathing scared the hell out of them.

"Are ya listening to me boy?" Gareth asked, sounding more than a little agitated.

"I'm sorry, Gareth," Conner said with a cringe. "My mind was wandering."

"Well, you'd best be paying attention. I said there is a young man watching us."

Conner scanned the room, being careful not to rest his eyes on the culprit. He was a tall, stout youth. His blue eyes darted around the room as if at any minute he were about to be caught doing something he shouldn't. It was this, more than anything else that told Conner that he was only a boy.

"He's headed this way," Conner replied, sipping his beer, "and our paranoid friend just grabbed her sword."

The boy walked right up to Gareth.

"Are you Gareth of Sersy?" he asked nervously.

"That depends mostly on who by asking." Gareth said, not bothering to look up.

"My name is Ross. My father is Duke Sheven. My brother..."

"We know who your brother was, boy. Sit." Gareth indicated the seat beside him and the nervous lad sat down. "What brings you here and without escort?"

"My father wished to know what befell my brother..."

"We don't know, lad," Conner said sadly. "Gareth and I and part of the troop were a day's ride ahead of the others. Trying to be a decoy..."

"Aye, what a mistake *that* was," Gareth muttered.

"By the time we decided there must be trouble and doubled back, they were all dead," Conner finished.

My father said there was a woman. A woman who saw everything."

"And remembers nothing," Gareth said. "She has been questioned by many people, many times. Your father himself questioned her. She doesn't remember."

Ross lowered his voice till he could only barely be heard. "My father has employed a sorceress who claims she can coax the memory from her."

"Sorceress," Gareth said beneath his breath. That explained what the boy was doing here, alone. Sorcery was something for the common folk. Considered by the gentry to be parlor tricks at best. No member of the nobility had employed a sorcerer for too long to be remembered. One doing such was likely to lose all credibility. So, the Duke had sent his son, who was not likely to gossip, for obvious reasons. He had sent him alone because alone he would excite no curiosity. Without escort, there was no way of knowing that he was any more than a boy out for a little adventuring.

"Rosanda is said to be the best. I, myself, have seen her do things which have no logical explanation." He lowered his voice again. "Truly *magical* things, my lord."

Gareth nodded. He had no trouble believing in magic. He'd seen enough of it in his time. He also knew that Conner was a firm believer. Shana was another story. Shana believed in nothing, save death and steel. Not since the attack. Not since her lover had been murdered and her face changed into a mask of mangled flesh.

Conner seemed to read his mind. "She'll never stand for it."

Ross gave them some incentive. "My father knows that this matter has marked your reputation and I can see by your manner of dress that your business is bad—"

"Why, you pompous, litte brat!" Conner made a move towards him and Gareth held up his arm to stop him.

"Calm, boy. It be true." He nodded at Ross. "Go on." Across the room, he saw Shana's hand twitch on her blade.

"If you find out who killed my brother, you'll also know who took the orb. If you could retrieve it, that would restore your reputation. In any case, my father is willing to pay you five hundred golds—"

"Enough said," Gareth smiled. "I shall see if I can persuade Shana."

YOU'VE GONE mad, Gareth." Shana looked up at him from where she sat on the bed. "You may believe in witches, but I do not. I can't see wasting my

time—"

"Shana, did you even hear me? Five hundred golds, whether it works or not. We're out of money. And if it *did* work, Shana . . . If we could get our reputation back . . ."

"There's about as much chance of that as there is of my getting my face back," she said bitterly.

"Okay, Shana, you win. But what about the gold?" Conner asked. "Don't be so damn selfish. How's the trip to Talgar going to hurt *you*? Will it cut into your self-pity time?"

Shana was instantly on her feet, sword in hand. "I'll slit you for that!"

Gareth stepped between them and raised his hand. "Calm down, the both of you," he ordered. He stared hard at Shana and she finally sheathed the sword. But she didn't sit down.

"It's easy for you to talk of going to Talgar," she hissed accusingly at Conner. "You lost *nothing* there."

"Yes, I did, Shana. I lost friends there. One of them was you. Maybe if we go back to Talgar . . . Maybe if we go back, you will find something more important than your face."

WE SHOULD be meeting up with the witch any time now," Gareth said. There was no reply from Shana. "Did you hear me?"

"My ears weren't damaged. Make him quit watching me, Gareth." She pulled the cloth back tight where it was beginning to sag. "That's all he's done for three days. Watch, watch, watch, every time I turn around he's staring at me. I swear, if he doesn't stop . . ."

"He's just a boy, Shana," Gareth said with a smile. "He never really knew Jered. It must be hard for him to understand why his brother would choose our lifestyle over theirs. Why he would choose you over a lady of the court."

"I doubt seriously that his curiosity stems from thoughts of his brother. Like everyone else, he wishes to know what horror lies behind this veil of cloth." She looked up, to see the youth once again watching her. "Damn him. He's doing it again. Have a word with him, Gareth. Make him stop or by night-fall I'll have his head."

Gareth sighed and nodded. He rode up even with Ross, who was a good two horse lengths ahead of them. Because of the distance, Gareth knew that Shana wasn't imagining things. In fact, it was no small wonder that young Ross could stay astride his horse. "I know you don't mean to, but you are provoking Shana's anger."

"How, my lord?" Ross asked, as he twisted in his saddle to look at Shana yet again.

"That's how," Gareth said, with a laugh. "You know, boy, you really shouldn't stare at someone who's deformed."

"Is that why she thinks I'm looking?" he blushed scarlet and muttered. "I wasn't even *trying* to look at her *face*."

Gareth laughed so hard he nearly fell off his mount and the boy blushed still redder. "She has a very nice body," Ross stuttered out.

Gareth stopped laughing. "That she does and she used to have a face that was more than a match for the body. A blade caught her across the face from hairline to chin. She's lucky to be alive, but I don't think Shana sees it that way."

"What do you mean?" At Ross's tender age, the concept of someone being better off dead was inconceivable.

"Shana exists. No more. No less. She has no god. She has no love. She shuns the thought of magic, because for her there is no magic. Shana used to enjoy the fight. I wish you could have seen her the day we . . ." he cleared his throat, "collected the orb." He smiled at memories of happier times. "She used to sing as we rode along." He laughed. "Hell, she used to sing in the middle of battle. She has a wonderful voice." His smile abruptly changed to a frown. "She never sings now. Yes, she used to enjoy the fight . . . Now all she cares about is the kill. It's the only thing that brings her real joy and that joy is gone as soon as the blood dries on her sword."

"You love her," Ross said and knew that his words were true.

Gareth looked as if he had been violated and he said with an edge of warning in his voice, "That sort of thing can get you into trouble, boy."

Ross watched in confusion as Gareth rode up to join Conner. So much was happening. He felt like he didn't know anything, but would soon.

THAT NIGHT, as they sat around the fire, the sorceress Rosanda stepped into the light. She was above average height, with long, black hair, fair skin and eyes so blue that they seemed to sear right through you. Her sturdy frame was covered from head to toe in long, white robes. She walked over and sat down at the fire as if she belonged.

The three men tried to act as if her presence had not startled them. Shana succeeded. She just sat there and looked at her finger nails, as if she had never seen anything quite as interesting and said, "That's a good way to get yourself killed."

"You must be Shana." Rosanda took Shana's insolence in stride. She'd cracked tougher nuts.

"What spell did you use to figure that one out?" Shana chided.

"Enough, Shana," Gareth turned to face Rosanda. "Please excuse our companion, my lady . . . ah, your high . . . ah . . ."

"Witch," Shana finished for him. "So, witch. Say 'wu ja wu ja' a couple of times, we'll all pick up our gold, and then—"

"This doesn't *have* to be difficult, Shana."

"It doesn't *have* to be easy, either." She stood abruptly. "Has it ever occurred to you that maybe I don't *want* to remember?" She turned and stomped off into the woods.

"Actually, I think that's exactly the problem," Rosanda said under her breath.

IN TWO days, they had reached their destination. An empty field a quarter day's ride out of the city of Talgar.

At the sorceress' request, Shana uncovered her face.

Ross was able to look without a single sign of emotion. It was obvious that Shana had indeed been a beautiful woman. But the blade had caught her above her right eye and hadn't stopped till it reached the left side of her chin. The right eye was a dual blue, and the pupil was white. The scar was deep and ragged. You could see each stitch, as if a drunk seamstress had sewn her up like an old rug. Her nose had been crushed and attempts to rebuilt it had not gone well. Yes, her face was a mess, but it was not unbearable.

"How will this work?" Gareth asked. He felt a sudden urge to bolt and run. Magic always had that effect on him.

"It won't," Shana said with a snide grin.

"That scar runs all the way into your soul," Rosanda said gently. "If you remembered nothing, that would be the case. If you remember anything at all, the spell will work. What you don't remember, the land will." She turned to address the rest of the party. "Shana will sit here, looking at the field. I will stand across from her and do what I must. Then we should all be able to see the events that took place in this spot on that night, two years ago."

Shana sat where she was told, and suddenly she had no more jokes. "Why did you sit me here?" she demanded.

"Because that's the place where you fell. That's where your blood spilled on the ground."

Shana stood up quickly. "I don't want to do this." She tried to move, but she couldn't. She looked at the sorceress in panic. Rosanda just smiled.

"It's okay, Shana, just sit down. It's too late to back out now." Rosanda went to take her place. Gareth grabbed her arm gently.

"It won't hurt her, will it?"

"If my hunch is right, it can't do anything but help her."

Rosanda took her place across from Shana. The words seemed to drift up out of her and soon a thick mist filled the whole area. As it cleared, they saw their camp. Two tents, a fire, their horses tethered out behind the tents. Except that they had yet to pitch camp and their horses were behind them.

Ross watched in fascination as his dead brother appeared. Then he frowned.

There was a small, glowing ball in his brother's left hand, which he quickly stuck in his pouch. In his right, he held his blade and it was covered with blood. He bent down and wiped it off on the grass.

"That son of a bitch," Conner hissed.

"Quiet," Gareth ordered.

Suddenly, Shana entered the camp. Not the Shana who sat on the edge of the field with a part of a face, but a whole Shana. Her blonde hair flowed loosely down around her shoulders. She turned and Ross saw her. His heart melted. Shana was indeed the most beautiful woman he had ever seen.

Shana walked towards Jered.

"See anything?" Jered asked.

"No, did you?"

Jered shook his head. "I think the night plays tricks on you, my love."

She looked around. "Aren't Heath and Mario back yet?"

"No," he said with a shrug. "I've been thinking, Shana. You know this orb thing . . . It's got to be worth a lot of money. Why don't we . . ."

She laughed, shaking her head. "You really are a demon, Jered. Can't you ever be happy?"

"No, I can't, Shana. My father's land should be mine, not William's. *I* should be the one to inherit. With a big enough guard and you to help me lead—"

"I have told you before and I'll tell you again. I have no desire to be a duchess. I have no wish to be any more than what I am. And much happier you would be if you felt the same way. I'm going to go look for the others. They should have been back by now."

"That's not a good idea, Shana." There was an ominous tone to Jered's voice. He raised his sword as Shana turned around. She looked at him and the expression on her face told the watchers that she knew she had been betrayed. "Jered . . . god's above! What have you done?" Shana whispered in horrified disbelief.

"Come with me, Shana, or stay here with them." He moved his sword into a striking position. "I don't want to kill you."

"I don't think you can." Even as she spoke, she was going for her sword. But before she could clear steel, he swung. The blade caught her face and threw her back, but she didn't lose her grip. She continued to draw and regained her footing. Jered's eyes widened in terror and Conner and Gareth knew why. Shana was the better swordsman. His only chance had been to catch her off guard and land the first blow. But the first blow had only slowed her down. Now she was going to kill him and he knew it.

"Shana—I'm sorry . . ." He managed to parry the first blow, but her second caught his throat and his blood hit the earth even before he did. But Shana didn't stop. She kept hacking at the twitching body until she reeled from loss of blood. The glint of light caught her eye. The orb lay where it had fallen, beside Jered's open pouch. She nearly fell on her face when she went to pick it up. The orb glowed brightly and then was gone.

Shana stumbled back and fell. As the old Shana touched the new Shana, the whole image disappeared.

"I killed Jered! *I* killed him," Shana started to cry and Gareth ran to comfort her. Conner went to help Rosanda, who seemed to be exhausted from her efforts.

Ross was incredulous. "My brother betrayed his friends with the hope of overthrowing my father. My brother lived and died a traitor. What on earth do I tell my father?"

"Where is the orb—and what the hell was it?" Conner demanded.

Rosanda held up her hand. "Please, let the questions wait till after I've rested."

THEY'D SET up camp, and they now sat around the fire drinking some peppermint tea which Rosanda had prepared for them.

The sorceress sat down and made herself comfortable with her tea. "I could answer some questions now."

"Did the orb make him do it?" Shana asked, staring deep into the heart of the fire.

"No, I'm sorry, but it was Jered's great greed which made him do it."

"What do I tell my father? He's an old man and not in the best of health. How can I tell him that my brother was a traitor and a murderer?" Ross was heart sick. He had made his brother into a mercenary hero. And now...

"Only the five of us know the truth. I suggest we tell him that it only helped us to locate the orb. Nothing can be gained by dragging Jered's name through the mud now." Rosanda looked at Gareth for confirmation.

"Agreed?" Gareth asked Conner and Shana. They nodded.

"As long as no one makes him a hero," Shana said bitterly.

"Not everyone you love will hurt you, Shana. Look at Gareth and Conner. They have stayed by your side in spite of the fact that you have made yourself impossible to live with."

Shana nodded. "I know that," she forced a smile. "Now."

"So, what is this orb and if you know where it is, please tell the rest of us," Conner said with some urgency.

"The orb belongs to my order. It was my order that hired you to . . . retrieve it . . . in the first place. I shall now return it to it's proper place. Of the orb itself, that is all you need to know. As to where the orb is . . ."

"I know," Ross said with a smile. He looked at Rosanda. "I know where it is."

"Where?" Rosanda asked with a skeptical lift of her brow.

"It's still in her hand," Ross said smugly.

Looking more surprised than skeptical, Rosanda smiled slightly and said, "Then go get it."

Ross walked over to Shana. "Hold out your hand, please."

She did and the orb appeared. He picked it up and took it to Rosanda, who quickly placed it into her pouch.

"I don't understand," Conner just shook his head in total confusion.

"Don't you see, Conner? It was there the whole time." Ross could see that Conner still didn't understand. "It was hiding." Conner just shrugged and Ross decided he was hopeless.

Rosanda sipped at her tea and relaxed, watching Shana with some satisfaction. Two years ago, this place just outside of Talgar had left its mark on Shana. Now it had done so a second time. ∎

The Spheres of Acamar

by Richard N. Dunbar, Sr.

The Acamarians were medical geniuses. Legend said they discovered the Elixer of Life on their once lush planet, but after a millenia, all that remained was a vast library of crystalline spheres. When the library was discovered, a horde of fortune hunters had descended on the dingy planet to try and decypher the spheres, but no one had succeeded. That was five years ago and the only ones left now were the die-hards and those who had spent all their money trying.

My last five thousand credits lay on the small round table before me. Maka, the alien owner of the sleazy casino, who looked more like a one-eyed octopus than anything else, had agreed to play me one-on-one in five card stud, a game he'd never played before. I hated dealing with him because I knew him for the slimeball he was, but this time, as in all the others, I had no choice.

Putting on my best poker face, I looked him in the eye and blew a puff of smoke in it just to irritate him. "You gonna fold or call?" I asked gruffly.

He blinked his one large yellow eye several times to clear the smoke as an electronic voice came over his expensive universal translator. "I don't think I like this game called poker, Earthling." His excuse for a mouth, a large orifice surrounded by hair and small wiggly things, didn't move in time with the words, like the soundtrack from a bad movie.

I held back a smile, partly because he didn't like the smoke and partly because I finally had him where I wanted him. "If you're not gonna match my bet then I win," I said, reaching for the sizeable pile of money on the table.

"Hold it!" Maka hissed, lashing onto my outstretched hand with one of his slithery tentacles. He waved a different one at a robot standing at the bar. "I'll throw in my bot to cover your five thousand credits."

The deal stank; big time. "Are you kidding? That bot must be fifty years old at least! That's ancient technology!" The bot was a humanoid model with the customary features but was obviously an old cold fusion powered unit. And one that hadn't been maintained in the best of conditions at that.

Maka smiled, at least I thought it was a smile, as he said, "I don't think I have to remind you who owns this joint, and *you* may have a rather large tab after this is over."

I glanced at his henchmen standing in the shadows of the smoky room just to make him think I was nervous. It wasn't hard to make out the yellow eyes of several tall tentacle-ridden thugs watching me carefully as I played with the boss. Since I was holding four kings, I agreed. "Okay, Maka. If you insist."

"I call," he said, releasing his cold grip.

We laid down our cards and I almost laughed when I saw his, but knew this wasn't the time. "I win," I said in an overly polite tone. His constant hissing grew noticeably louder. "I have to be going now, Maka." I pushed back my chair and stood to rake the money in.

"Wait, Earthling! I want to play one of *my* games now!"

"I'm sorry," I said with a curt smile, "I have to see a friend about a ship." Quickly stuffing the money into any pocket I could find, I motioned to the bot. "Come on, bot, let's go."

The bot turned his metallic head towards me and then to Maka, unsure of what he should do. When he didn't move, I gave Maka an irritated frown, "If you don't mind." I didn't need the bot since I had won more than enough to make it home, I just wanted to take Maka for all I could in return for all the times he had taken me. Although it would never make us even, every little bit helped.

It was clear Maka didn't want me to

go, but after eyeing his other customers, he reluctantly growled at the bot, "Go ahead. You belong to him now."

"Thank you," I said and spun around to head straight for the door.

Outside Maka's place, I hit the dimly lit dusty street on the run. "Come on bot, let's got out of here!" I called out over my shoulder.

He broke into a trot several steps behind me and raised his voice so I could hear it. "Why are we running, sir?"

"Maka doesn't like to lose. In there, he has a reputation to keep, but out here, we're on our own!" I glanced back at the casino in time to see two dark shapes slither out the alley door. "They're after us! I'm not waiting for ya!" I cried, breaking into an all-out dash for my speeder. I was surprised when the bot pulled ahead of me; evidently he understood.

In full stride, I wrestled the remote control from my pocket and pounded the keys. I could see the cockpit open up and just prayed the engine had started as well. As we vaulted in, I yelled, "Hold on!" and slammed the vertical throttle to full power without closing the hatch. The speeder shot straight up in the air and the dark shapes converged on the spot where we had been. With a flick of a switch, I closed the hatch and looked over at the bot who appeared to be holding on for dear life. "Somethin' wrong, bot?"

"Want me to drive?" was his weak reply.

I just smiled and punched the main thrusters to full power.

THE SOUND of heavy pounding on the door to my seedy bungalow woke me up. "Hold on a minute!" I slipped my blaster out from underneath my pillow. I didn't know how he had found me, but I knew who was on the other side of the door.

"Shall I get that, sir?" the bot asked from his seat in the far corner of the room.

My jaw dropped at the question; this bot couldn't possibly be *that* stupid. "Are you crazy?" Getting out of bed as quietly as possible, I silently waved the bot towards the back window and called out, "Who's there?" Before I had taken another step, the door burst open and the chain fell in little pieces to the floor. The bot and I froze in our tracks.

"Sere iss sree of uss," the leader sibilated as I stared down the barrels of three blasters.

"Whadda ya want?" I growled.

"Maka wanss hiss money back," the leader hissed.

"I won it fair and square!"

The leader waved his gun at the bot. "Maka sinks see bos iss worsh more san five sousand crediss. Give uss see money and you can keep see bos."

Not liking the deal, I tried a different one. "How 'bout *I* keep the money and *you* get the bot?"

"No!" was his emphatic reply.

I didn't know what to do. Two I could handle, but three was pushing it. And they were big ones at that. The bot was still frozen and I knew he wouldn't be any help; his synaptic brain was slave to the three laws of robotics. We stood there pointing our guns at each other for several long seconds until it occurred to me that they would rather die than face Maka's wrath. Having no other choice, I cautiously put my gun down on the bed.

The sleazy creatures searched me and took all the cash I had won and then some. I knew the surplus would never make it into their master's hands. After they left, taking my gun with them, I kicked the bed and made many unpleasant remarks about Maka's lineage as the pain in my foot subsided.

"I don't think Maka *has* a mother, sir," the bot said innocently from his chair in the corner of the bare room.

I let out a quick laugh. "No, I'm sure you're right."

My smile faded quickly as I sat down on the edge of the bed. Here I was, flat broke, no job, and the chances of getting out any time soon had suddenly gotten slimmer than filling an inside straight. Eyeing the bot, I wondered how much he'd fetch on the open market. "Got any *gold* components in you, bot?" I asked gruffly.

"I can *assure* you that I'm worth more to you as an assistant than as spare parts, sir," the bot said earnestly.

After thinking about it, I groaned, "You're probably right. If Maka doesn't want you, you've *got* to be worthless." I cast a disgusted glance at the expressionless metallic face of the bot who suddenly became very still. Everything was going just fine until this bot came into the picture. "You're bad luck, ya know that?" He just sat there and didn't say a word.

I took out a cigarette and started to search around for matches when suddenly, the bot was in my face, his finger on fire. "Need a light, sir?"

"Oh, thanks," I said and lit my cigarette. Blowing a puff, I carefully watched the bot return to his seat to resume his motionless stare. Since I didn't have anything left to lose, I thought I'd see what he had in mind. "An assistant, heh? How can *you* help *me*?"

He was quick to say, "There must be at least a *dozen* ways."

"Name one," I grunted.

Although he finally moved, it seemed to be more like a squirming motion. "Like ... like ..." and then his tone changed to an inquisitive one, "What *exactly* do you do for a living, sir?"

I sighed since he was obviously winging it. "I'm a computer systems analyst."

"Ah! Then you would be after the formula for the Acamarian Elixer of Youth," he said, bobbing his head in confidence.

"Yeah, that's right," I replied, unimpressed. "Just about everybody on this rock is."

"Then I can help you search for it."

I didn't say anything else as I started to get dressed. The bot watched patiently and had the good sense to keep quiet. He had cost me a bundle and I could forget ever getting it back. Since I was stuck with him anyway, I reluctantly decided to give him a chance. "Well, I can't keep calling you *bot* all the time, do you have a nickname?" I asked, zipping up my suit.

"Well . . . Maka used to call me Robb."

"Robb?" It sounded devious, just like something the sleazy octopus would come up with. "Where'd *Robb* come from?"

The bot hesitated, then cautiously answered, "It stood for Rusty Old Bit Bucket, sir."

I let out a laugh. "Okay, Robby it is."

ROBBY AND I stood alone in the dusty underground Acamarian library, looking down the seemingly infinite rows of glass cases. The place had been excavated several years ago and nobody cleaned it anymore. Each see-through case had several glass shelves and each shelf contained thirty perfectly round crystalline spheres, neatly lined up in three rows. The overhead lights would've made the crystals sparkle if the place hadn't been so dusty. "There must be millions of them," Robby said, his voice hushed.

"Over five."

Suddenly, he started looking around and rubbed his hands together like he was getting ready for business. "Where's the computer interface?"

My mouth fell open at the question as I gave him an incredulous look. "Rusted away, *Robb*." I thought I saw him flinch at his former name.

"Rusted away?" he asked, uneasily shifting his weight to the other foot.

"Yeah, the only things left are the spheres," I replied, waving an exasperated hand at the cases.

Staring down the rows, he became motionless and murmured, "This could be more difficult than I thought." He turned to face me. "Mind if I ask a few questions, sir?"

"Go ahead," I said with a shrug. I certainly didn't have anything better to do.

Anxious for the answer, he cocked his head to one side. "What makes you think the formula really exists and if so, why do you think it's in these spheres?"

I was beginning to like his attitude so I eased up on him. "I don't *know* if it exists, nobody does. I came here five years ago to find out and spent all my money trying. At this point, I'm just trying to figure out a way to get back to a starbase."

"I see."

With a sigh, I started to ramble. "Yeah, there aren't many jobs on this planet for a computer systems analyst, other than looking for the formula." I sat down on a chair next to one of the crystalline cases and folded my arms as I leaned back to relax. "Anyway, to answer your second question, the rest of the ruins have been searched over and over again, and *nothing's* ever turned up. The problem is that it's been so long, everything's turned to ru—" catching myself, I changed the word for his sake, "—ah, dust. If the formula exists, it's in those spheres."

Robby gazed down the rows. "Can you tell me what's already been tried to read them?"

"No," I frowned in dismay. "The list's too long."

He motioned to a nearby case. "Mind if I look at one?"

"Of course not." I reached over to pick one out, blew the dust off, and handed it to him gingerly. "Here, take a look."

Taking the sphere, he started to turn it in various angles to see the different patterns within. As I watched in silence, it suddenly occurred to me that he was turning the sphere the same way, over and over again. "I think I can read it, sir," he replied, turning the sphere as he looked into it.

I was stunned. "Really?" This couldn't be true! Five long years I had labored at trying to read them and this bot had done it in five *minutes*? But human bots don't lie, not to humans anyway.

"Yes, sir."

"But how?"

He rattled out the facts, "The information in this sphere has been put there using polarized laser light."

I stood up to get a closer look at the sphere in his hand. "You mean holographics?"

"That would be a crude analogy, sir, but not as advanced as that."

All *I* could see was a bunch of fuzzy patterns, so I was a little skeptical. "But how can *you* read it?"

He continued to stare at the sphere as he rotated it in his hands. "Two factors. First is that my vision is magnified—"

"We tried that."

". . . and the second is that I have stereoscopic vision."

I started to get excited when I realized what he was talking about. "The fact that you have *two* eyes."

"Yes, sir. You see, the polarized images are superimposed on each other to give the sphere a higher information capacity."

"Of course! Why didn't I think of this before? We always used a *single* optical reader."

Robby's eyes were glued to the sphere which he continued to turn around, like he was juggling it. "However, it will take a very long time at this rate. If I could spin the sphere at thirty thousand revolutions per second I could maximize the transfer rate, sir."

Immediately, my brain started to tick. "Hmm. That's fast. We'll need to get some parts." I thought I noticed him flinch at the word 'parts' so I added, "Not yours," in an assuring tone.

He said, "This one's a math book." But I wasn't listening. I was thinking about how to get the money to build the spinner.

I rambled on, "The trick's gonna be gettin' the money without letting Maka know what's goin' on."

I HATED the smell of Maka's place, it reminded me of dead fish. He was sitting in his porcelain tub in his private office, and insisted that I lie on my back in the middle of the dusty floor; the customary position for asking favors from 'The Great Maka'. "What do you want, Earthling?" He continued without waiting for a reply, "I say the bot's worth five thousand, do you disagree?"

"It's not about the bot," I replied with a hurt look. "I need a loan."

Maka smiled, I think. "You know your credit's always good with me. How much this time?"

"Ten thousand."

"*Ten* thousand?" he asked, his eye opening wider at the amount.

Sensing his suspicion, I made something up and pretended to be irritated about it. "Yeah, that five thousand credit bot of mine needs some parts."

He chuckled in a hissing sort of way. "Okay, ten thousand it is."

FOR THE next few days, I bought parts and built the spinner as Robby worked on cracking the Acamarian language. Just as I finished the spinner, he cracked it. Fortunately, the first sphere I had picked out was on mathematics, a universal language. He told me that any other sphere would've probably taken him months to figure out. With the language problem solved, we moved the spinner to a secluded spot in the library and went to work reading the spheres. Soon after, we found the medical section and finally, the formula itself.

There was only one more problem to solve, and that was how to get off this crummy planet. I groaned when I realized that meant more money, and more money meant Maka. I knew I'd have a hard time selling the formula to him because although *I* didn't mind sharing, I didn't think *he* would. The less competition, the more profits, he always said.

Turning to Robby, I ordered, "Store

the formula in your permanent memory and lock it under my voice."

"Yes, sir."

"Under *no* condition are you to give it to anyone or even let them know you have it."

"Yes, sir. You can count on me, sir," he said, bobbing his head enthusiastically. I could tell he was delighted to be so entrusted.

ONCE AGAIN I found myself lying on my back in Maka's smelly office, my eyes glued to the ceiling. He was soaking in his tub, waiting for me to say something, but I took my time since I had the upper hand.

"What do you want, Earthling?" he asked, taking a loud sip from his frothy drink.

"I want to sell you something," I said innocently.

"I'm not buying the bot," was his gruff reply.

I smiled to myself since it was Robby who had done everything. "It's not the bot. It's a certain Acamarian sphere."

Maka froze with his drink halfway to his mouth, his single eye opened wide. "You found it?" he gasped.

"Yeah." I continued to stare at the ceiling, pretending not to notice.

"*And* you figured out how to read it?"

I nodded as best I could, given that my head was on the floor. I couldn't tell him the whole truth, but I had to be believable. "Yeah, I did it with a polarized light reader."

He was silent only for a moment and then snapped, "How much?" as if his back was against the wall.

Prepared for the question, I replied, "The price of two tickets outta here plus

ten thousand." When I remembered my current debt, I quickly added, "And you forget the ten I already owe you."

" *Two* tickets?"

"I'm taking the bot with me."

"Why?" he asked suspiciously.

I had an answer I knew he'd buy. "I know a good metallurgist who'll pay well."

And he did. "Consider it done, Earthling."

Getting up to dust myself off, I looked him in that one yellow eye of his. "There is one other thing. I'm gettin' outta here alive, Maka."

"But of course."

Shooting him an irritated glance as I slapped the dust off my pants, I retorted, "Don't give me that, I know you too well. I'm not giving you the sphere until I'm standing on the ramp to the shuttle. You won't do anything with all those people watching."

He grunted. "Is that it?"

I thought about it for several seconds, but I couldn't think of anything else; at least, nothing I thought he'd go for. "Yeah, that's it."

Maka firmly set his drink down to give me his full attention. "I'll agree to your terms," he pointed a tentacle at me, "but, you must give me the reader *and* you must prove to me that it works."

The spinner was the first thing that popped into my mind. "Okay."

I WAS standing in the center of the room with a sphere in each hand when Maka showed up with two of his kin folk. They closed the door a little too quickly so I extended an arm and dropped one. As it shattered into a thousand pieces on the floor, I gave him a sly smile. "See how easily they break, Maka?"

He motioned his thugs away from Robby and the spinner.

"*That* was a collection of celestial charts." I nodded at the pieces on the floor and held up the remaining sphere. "No tricks, Maka, or this one goes."

"Okay, Earthling," he growled, his eye glued to my hand.

It was easy getting Maka to believe that the spinner was actually the reader. What he didn't know was that Robby had provided the data to the recorder, not the spinner. Since there wasn't any way I was going to give him the whole formula until I was safe, we only fed half of it to the recorder; enough for him to know it was genuine.

Right after we finished the recording, one of his thugs took the spinner off somewhere while Maka and the other escorted us to the space terminal. In the speeder, I wasn't sure if I'd be able to break the sphere, so I took out my blaster and pointed it at it. Since *I* had to have a drawn blaster, *Maka* had to have one too, and that just made everyone nervous. After we checked our guns at the terminal entrance, the tension eased up a bit.

We sure got some strange looks when I strolled through the crowded terminal with my arm extended, as if I were sleep-walking. Maka had watched me put the sphere in a small bag so nobody would know what it was, but I wouldn't let him near it. When we reached the ramp to the shuttle, I stopped and eyed the tentacle wrapped around my other arm. "Okay, you can let go now, Maka."

"Give me the bag and I will."

"No can do," I said with a shake of my head.

"If I let you go, you'll take it so you can have it all to yourself!"

I was relieved that either he didn't know I already had the formula or didn't care. "No, I won't, I give you my word." I was pretty sure he'd buy it since I had always paid back my loans, along with his outrageous interest.

Hissing slightly, he reluctantly released his grip. "Okay, Earthling. But if you try anything, I'll destroy the shuttle before it reaches orbit."

I started pushing Robby up the ramp to move him along faster. At the door to the shuttle, I turned and gently tossed the bag to Maka who snatched it out of the air with four or five of his tentacles. After inspecting the contents, he nodded his head in satisfaction and quietly slithered away into the crowd, followed by his thug. I strolled through the shuttle door and the attendant closed it securely behind me.

WE WERE sitting in our seats on the starship, watching through the window as the shuttle returned to the planet below. We were safe and there was nothing Maka could do about it now. I had just finished giving Robby a friendly lecture on 'supply and demand' when he turned to ask, "I guess it's too bad you had to give the sphere to Maka. Since he has more money than you, he'll be able to produce more than you and flood the market."

"Oh, it's not so bad," I said, smiling..

"But didn't you tell him about the polarized light?"

"Of course, but he'll never crack it." My smile broke into a grin since I knew we were finally even. "You see, since Maka's race has only *one* eye, he'd never think of using *two* in a million years." Robby seemed to be puzzled so I added, "Or at least not before *I* flood the market." ∎

The Hunter

by Gerard Daniel Houarner

Beasts howled. Branches snapped. Lightning stabbed at the hilltops; thunder echoed through the valleys. The earth trembled under galloping hooves and paws.

Crowen looked over his shoulder as he ran blindly into the light. He tripped over an exposed tree root, then stumbled against a trunk. Rough bark scratched his palms and cheek.

"Run, run, Crowen of Fech," the spirit within the tree whispered. It laughed. "The Hunt is loose this night. Do you hear, do you hear?"

"Shut up!" Crowen spun away from the tree, rushed on through the darkness.

A gust of wind raised dead leaves. Its chill hand slapped Crowen across the face, ruffling his long hair. When the gust died, the sounds of the pursuing beasts and the approaching storm were gone. Clouds parted suddenly. A full moon framed by storm gazed down on Crowen.

Is it time for the full moon already? Crowen asked himself. What day— what month is this—

His thought froze when he could not hear his own words though he spoke aloud. Then the moon spoke.

"Rest, Crowen of Fech," said the moon.

Crowen's legs gave out and he collapsed into a bed of mushrooms. The moon's voice was soft, gentle. It reminded Crowen of the Court orphan caretaker's tone when he was a child and she wanted to comfort him and lure him back into the sleep he had just fled, the sleep where nightmares waited.

"Give yourself to the dead," the moon continued. "It will go easier for you. Go below, child, and flee the lands of the living. There are worse things than the dead searching for you this night."

He sank his fingers through a carpet of leaves and touched the soil. The pungent stench of decay rolled over him. His hand closed over the rotted body of a small, red-beaked bird. The corpse fell apart in his grip, and scavenging insects and worms scattered under his hand. Tears suddenly burned his eyes, blurring his vision. The Hunt was after him. What was he doing out on a full moon? Why had the Huntsman chosen him? He was innocent, he had done nothing. Nothing.

The moon withdrew behind clouds while rain fell in waves through the bare branches overhead. The beasts of the Hunt bayed at the vanished moon, then barked and snarled as they took up his scent. The earth shuddered once more beneath their gallop; the woods crackled as furred and armored bodies crashed through the underbrush. The wind howled, thunder roared. The Huntsman's horn sang a mournful note that chilled Crowen.

His legs found strength in fear. He stood and pushed himself up a slope. Slipping on rain-soaked leaves, he slid one step for every two he took. The sounds of the Hunt faded; a distant horn urged the beasts on. Crowen cried out as he sank to his hands and feet and scrambled uphill. Legend said the Hunt was at its quietest when closing on its prey.

Cold stone against his fingers startled him. Markings carved in the rock told him he had come to a tomb set into the hill. Crowen pushed and pulled at the stone marker until it moved. He thought of the damp, cool darkness behind the stone and hoped there was enough room for him. Perhaps, if he covered himself with the corpse and threw the grave offerings over the dust he disturbed, the Hunt would not find him.

He had pushed the marker half-way across the opening when a voice, hollow like a distant echo, spoke from within.

"Who tries this gate?"

"What? Who speaks?" Crowen shouted. His hands fell away from the marker, and from habit reached for his dagger scabbard. His fingers clutched at the empty scabbard and finally balled into fists. He crouched, ready to launch himself at whoever came through the narrow crack in the earth.

A fine cloud of dust blew out with the stale, musty air. "A fellow traveller, it would seem," said the voice. A figure slipped through the breach. "Though at least I know the road we're both on."

Lightning flashed, illuminating dried flesh and a linen gown hanging in tatters from the figure's gaunt frame. Pale bone and yellowed teeth glowed from between strips of blackened flesh.

"I'm no fellow to you," Crowen protested, fear adding venom to his words. As if to prove his point, he started to scan his attire, and stopped. His trousers were torn from split boots to crotch. His shirt of fine cloth and close stitching was pierced and torn, each hole marked with dark stains.

"I know you," the skeletal figure said, then floated closer to Crowen. It stuck a bony finger through one of the holes in his shirt. The finger went through cloth skin, bone, and tickled something inside Crowen's body.

"Should have kept your guard up," the figure said. It laughed, and Crowen flinched at its foul breath. "Of course, we all should have kept our guard up around you."

Fists unclenching, Crowen took a step back. His arms, suddenly heavy, sank like weights to his sides. What had happened to his clothes, to his body? Why was the Hunt after him? How could he talk to the dead? He kept the questions to himself, afraid that the corpse might answer him. He did not look at the hole through which the corpse's finger penetrated him. Instead, he tried to remember his life before the moment he had heard the cry of the Hunt in the valley below. Nothing came. Before the moment he understood he was being pursued, he might never have lived.

"We think of you in the world below, Crowen of Fech," the figure said. After withdrawing its finger, the figure wagged it in Crowen's face. "You were so young, so daring. Such a sight on your fine strong horse, riding in on the road from your precious Queen's land, carrying a satchel of books and scrolls for Father, a sword for my brother Tempou, and for me, that smile, those eyes. For me, sweet Crowen of Fech, you carried a mask."

Crowen's heart raced. He glanced at the stone marker, but could not make out the name. He started to back away, then stopped. Shadows lurked between the trees. Low growls, snuffling, hisses and grunts mingled with the wail of wind through bare branches. Crowen froze. It came to him that he was dead, and that the moon had been right. There were worse things after him than spirits of the dead.

"Don't you remember me, Crowen of Fech? You said I was the star that called you across the waters, the light that drove away the darkness in your heart. Don't you remember your sweet Mithete?"

"Mithete?" Crowen whispered. The name was a haunting. It brought back a melody made on cool, romantic evenings; sweet words framed by music forged in his soul.

The fear of something that might strike deeper than any pain the Hunt could inflict on a soul coiled like a venomous snake in the pit of his stomach.

"For a year you wooed me, Crowen. Remember the songs you sang? You made the wood spirits sigh and the hill dwarves dance around their stone circles. Soft words you always had, and how refreshing they were in this harsh land of warriors and farmers. I never noticed the poison you slipped in your songs about beautiful daughters wronged by their fathers and brave sons held back by jealous elders. But then, you knew my brother and I were eager for your sweet poison. I never hated my father more than the night you told the tale of Geyod murdering his wife for the rights to a kingdom. I wept for my dead mother, and knew with no more proof than anyone else had that she had not died from a weak heart. You made me believe father had her murdered."

"Mithete." The name was an ache within him. He remembered long, auburn hair and a quick smile; hands like doves gliding through the air; warm, soft skin. He remembered his voice and harp, inspired by Mithete, finding new ranges to explore and make his own. The memories, and the music, belonged to a life he once had.

Lightning struck a nearby tree. In the cold, white flash of light he saw only a few dry strands of hair sticking out from the blackened flesh covering her skull. Hands like dead ravens, flesh cold, there was only a smile left to remind him of what she had been. A terrible smile.

Crowen caught a glimpse of something moving beside him. A paw tipped with silver talons reached out to him from behind a tree trunk. A chill breeze blew rhythmically against the back of his neck. Without turning around, Crowen took a step towards the tomb.

"The Queen explained it to me, down below," Mithete said, cocking her skull to the side and placing a bony finger on the corner of her ragged mouth. "It seems that you actually did fall in love with me. Or perhaps, it was only the idea of loving someone other than yourself that you came to cherish. We debate that point, the Queen and I."

"I—I'm sorry, Mithete." His voice was a dry croak.

"Your tongue's out of practice, Crowen. In days gone by, you would have offered a clever tale held together by a dash of charm and a handful of sly half-truths. The years carrying the burden of all our curses have not been kind to you."

The rain stopped, but the lightning and thunder intensified, as if the hill had become the storm's center. Tall, hunch-backed beasts with matted grey fur loped among the trees, circling the tomb, keeping yellow, baleful eyes on him. Their snarls and hoof-beats were nearly drowned by peals of thunder. Two low notes grumbled through the night, dragged by the Huntsman's horn out of terrible depths.

Memories shook themselves free of the darkness in Crowen's mind. He recalled a marble court, velvet hangings, a throne, a four-posted bed of dark wood that held a soft mattress. The queen, older than he, her golden hair touched with grey, had favored the young, orphaned court singer and invited him to join her intrigues. Had he really been so proud? Had he really believed the queen would keep her promise to elevate him from his station as a court entertainer if he seduced Mithete, daughter of a distant lord; sowed dissent in her father's uneasy family; and fostered rebellion in the lord's castle?

"I tried to end the plot," Crowen offered. He tentatively held out a hand palm up, afraid Mithete might take it in her grasp.

"I know. And quite a scene it was, I'm told. Tempou on one side, screaming about how you had driven him to kill our father to avenge our mother's supposed murder. The queen's captain on the other, laughing at your arrogance, your toying with a queen's affection. As if you had been the only spy in the castle. Swords on either side, and not a sympathetic ear around. You needed me at that moment, didn't you? A pity you had already slain me."

"An accident, I swear. The dagger, it was meant for the captain. When I saw him at the gate, leading that pack of rebels, I recognized him from court. I was looking for him. In the castle. You took me by surprise, I didn't mean to stab—"

"You can imagine *my* surprise, Crowen. Father a bloody heap in the armory, rebels and foreign warriors streaming through our castle, Tempou blind with fury. All I wanted was a last moment of peace with you. At least my people didn't forget me—they gave me such a nice tomb." She turned, raised a hand. The stone marker tumbled to the side. A soft light began to glow from within. Wisps of luminescent fog rolled out along the ground and down the hillside. "Father's is further up, next to mother's. The plot your queen weaved came undone soon after those rebels took the castle. The kitchen maid's cache of poisons was discovered, and she confessed to being mother's assassin. She was just another of your queen's agents. The maid's torture was quite exquisite, so she's told us, and her inquisitors were a bit put off to find father innocent. But at least honor was restored to the family, and mother and father are together above as they are below. Even your queen received a grand funeral. She's quite pleased with the work surgeons performed on what was left of her face after one of my cousins pushed a tower stone down on her head. Yours, well, the people dragged your body to the woods and let wolves have it. I suppose you should count yourself lucky our curses caught your spirit before the wolves had a chance to mangle it even more. Your quite a sight, as it is."

The fog rolled through Crowen's legs like gentle surf, then stopped. Misty tendrils lapped at his knees. He touched the tears in his shirt. The dull impact of metal on flesh and bone came back to him, and he almost crumpled and fell to his knees from the memory of the blows that had killed him.

"But I don't blame you for forgetting me, Crowen. How could I? That was my dying curse on you, that you should lose every happy moment we shared together. The queen, she only wished you'd forget how to love when she heard of your attempted betrayal. Father's the one who cursed your soul to wander his land, friendless, with no past or future. He never trusted you, but he was afraid that if he interfered, he'd lose us completely. He was a good lord, a good father. You see things differently after you die. He never did anything to hurt mother, never did anything to earn our hate. Tempou and I, we deserved you. But father did not."

The light from the tomb grew brighter and spread until the grave site was lit by the incandescent fog. At the light's periphery, the beasts still capered in silence.

"And Tempou?" Crowen asked. "What did he wish on me?"

Mithete hesitated, turned her head. "My brother chose another path."

The song he had made about Tempou ran through his mind. Though he had weaved a tale about fierce warriors raging over stolen rights and avenging family betrayals, he had been surprised when the parts Tempou most favored in public had featured victorious warriors being merciful to defeated foes. Crowen had considered Tempou's concern for mercy an affectation to soften his reputation among women. Now he wondered if he had not tapped a hidden vein of gentleness in Mithete's brother. He hoped the path Tempou had chosen was mercy. "Then what do you want from me now?" Crowen asked, shifting nervously from one foot to the other.

"The dead are weary of carrying the burden of their curses. Mother has forgiven the queen for all the plotting and deaths, and father has forgiven his children for their betrayal. We want our peace."

"You forgive me?" Hope gave Crowen the courage to take another step towards her.

"No. Your years of wandering have taught you nothing. Without love, without memory, you were spared the torment of knowing your deeds. But you will have your peace. After the queen exacts a more suitable vengeance, and father and mother. And I, of course. We all have a price to take from you."

"Are you mad?" Crowen withdrew, trying to escape the fog which continued to cling to his legs. "You want me to submit to your torments?"

"We hunger for justice, and you must suffer before our appetites can be satisfied. But I promise, the spirits waiting for you will find peace in time. And when we find ours, you will find yours. Come join the dead, Crowen of Fech. Leave this world of the living behind. It is not a place for you. There is suffering here that will never end."

"So you say," said Crowen as he stepped beyond the fog's boundary. The light in the tomb flickered as figures moved back and forth across the entrance. They beckoned for him to join them. "I loved you then, Mithete. And I'm sorry for the suffering I caused. But I don't love you anymore. And I don't care about your hunger for justice. Your appetites are not mine. There's no reason for me to go down there."

"Don't you want to meet your parents?" she said, and two dark figures crowded towards the tomb entrance, nearly blocking the light. "Childhood friends from court? Lovers?" Other figures pushed across the entrance, shifting shadows obscuring their features. "They're all there, and many more. We are company, at least. There are no friends for you up here."

Crowen shook his head. "I have no interest in my parents; they didn't live long enough for me to know them. Friends I never had as a child, and lovers were only toys for me. Songs were the only things I've cared about, the only things that brought me joy. Those I can sing just as well here. No, Mithete. I will not go."

Mithete drifted towards the tomb entrance. The fog receded, the glow faded. "Those around us will take you if you do not come with me. You would not like to be taken."

Crowen felt a surge of confidence flow through him as he remembered, and savored, old triumphs from his living days: the moment's silence at court after he sang particularly well; the laughter he provoked with his fool's tales; the visiting dignitaries he tricked with his glib tongue into believing his role in court was greater than what it appeared to be. He remembered seducing women who hated him, and the jealous rivals and husbands he appeased. There had been duels he had won without lifting a weapon, and powers he had raised without spells. He remembered the joy of his art.

"I've been asleep, but you have awakened me, Mithete," said Crowen, with a slight bow. "I thank you for the gift of bringing life back to the dead. I don't fear the Hunt. They won't catch me. You've given me what I need to find a way out of danger, and a way to find my peace. I hope you will find yours."

"Our appetites will find satisfaction and we will have our peace," said Mithete as she disappeared into the darkness of her tomb. "But not all the dead find serenity so easily. Farewell."

The fog rolled back into the tomb and the glow was extinguished. A fine rain began to fall. Thunder rolled into the distance and lightning lost the trail to earth.

The marker glided back over the entrance.

An icy breeze blew once more against the back of his neck. Clawed shadows broke free from clustered trees. Scales clattered, grunting and hissing shapes shot past him. The air became tainted by the smell of wet fur. The running forms drew a tighter circle around him. Silently, the Hunt came upon him.

He opened his mouth, ready to sing, words falling together in his mind over a mournful tune. The circle of beasts, furred and scaled, horned and spiked, parted for a moment. Crowen held his breath.

A caped and hooded figure mounted on a massive black horse, with dark veins pulsing though its flanks were ripped and its collar bone lay exposed, came through the circle and stopped. Crowen fixed his gaze on the sword across the figure's lap. It was the sword he had given Tempou.

"Please," said the figure in a hoarse whisper, "proceed."

The words and music fled before Crowen's sudden panic. He took a deep breath and tried to summon the poetry back, but found only an emptiness like a silent, night-shrouded meadow frozen in the moment before sunrise. He had sung for his life before, he told himself, and he had faced supernatural powers. Where was the song?

The horse snuffled and cold, blue flames erupted from the beast's nostrils.

"Noble Lord," Crowen began, forgetting poetry and music, reaching simply for thoughts and words, "for years you could not find me, could not drag me back to the dead lands. For years I escaped you, and I was not even aware I was eluding you. What would happen if I made songs of this, if I made a fool of you among the living and the dead? Would you still be proud, sitting there on your fearsome horse? Would you and your beasts still command the respect and fear of the living

and the dead?"

"The Hunt," the figure whispered, "has changed."

Crowen laughed nervously. "Is death no longer death? Life no longer life?"

The figure held up the sword with a grey, emaciated hand. "You know this weapon?"

A denial came to his lips, but Crowen forced it back. Finally, fearfully, he named the figure. "Tempou."

Low laughter trickled over the long, harsh growls coming from either side of Crowen. "Old friend," the figure said as it lowered the hood. "Where are your songs, now?"

Tempou's face, criss-crossed with cuts, glowed with a soft, green radiance. Dried blood crusted the wounds, the lips, the corners of his eyes. Matted hair hung in clumps from his scalp. Unlike his sister, Tempou did not smile at Crowen.

Crowen stared at the sword. Memories sparked to life, flared into the details of Tempou's character. The old songs he had made for Tempou returned, but Crowen did not sing them. That would be too obvious, bring back too many bad feelings, he thought. But he was certain there was a song to be made for his old friend that would appeal to his sense of mercy.

"What took you so long to catch up to me?" Crowen asked boldly.

Tempou pulled a rein and kicked, driving the horse into a sidestepping circle around Crowen. "The curses protected you," he said as misshapen beasts with the long-snouted heads of hounds and the flat skulls and bulging eyes of snakes made way for him. "But no longer. The Hunt is free to take you."

"Back to the dead."

"The Hunt of old would do so. This is a new Hunt."

Crowen turned to keep Tempou in sight. "A song to the new Hunt, then, my old friend," he said lightly, hoping to cut through Tempou's grim mood with an appeal to past camraderie. "And to old pains."

A tune, sad but not grieving, lifted Crowen's opening words to the Huntsman. He sketched youthful characters in a pastoral setting, making sure to include all of Tempou's favorite flowers, trees, and animals. A tragic war filled the background, and Crowen lingered over brave deeds and heroic fights to make certain he had Tempou's attention. Using his hands to accent the action and lure Tempou further into the story-telling spell, he went on to tell of love setting friends against each other, jealousies leading to betrayals, tragic choices made in youthful haste. The characters spun secret plots that gathered speed and power, until the entire countryside was in arms and smoke blackened the sky. Crowen had half the cast killed and the rest dispersed, lost in far lands, friendless and lonely. He was careful that his characters not ask for mercy, but rather accept the punishment of wandering the earth in exile. At the song's end, he planted a trace of hope in the tune, trying to leave a final sense of satisfaction in the completion of the tale.

Crowen shivered after he finished. Beasts of the Hunt whined and panted softly all around him. Not a single baleful eye met his gaze. With a surge of confidence, Crowen looked up expectantly at Tempou. There was no change in Tempou's expression, and his grip on the sword had not loosened.

"I do not care for the song," the Hunt's master whispered.

The beasts began growling at Crowen once more.

"Perhaps I've chosen a poor subject," Crowen said quickly. His voice sounded high, his words stumbled over each other. "Forgive me, old friend. The years . . . we haven't seen each other for so long . . . tell me, what does your heart need to hear? You know my skills, you know I can please you. Let me do what I can to ease the burden you bear."

"I have only one need, and I have satisfied it now. With you."

Wary, Crowen asked, "What service may I perform?"

"Suffer," Tempou whispered. "You have the memories now, the love, greed, vanity and fear that destroyed my family. There's enough in you to suffer."

"That's not the Huntsman's task," Crowen protested. "You must bring me to the land of the dead."

"No."

Shock made Crowen stutter. "No? Then where would you bring me?"

"Across the world. Up to the stars. Wherever you lead us. The Hunt is yours now. It chases you. Chews you up and pukes you out, to start over again. There will never be any rest, for you or me. My sould can never know rest for what I allowed, for what I did."

"Where is the Huntsman of legend?" Crowen shouted desperately. "You fail at the task he was set to do."

"You misunderstand, old friend," said Tempou, leaning forward against his mount's neck. "You did more than lead me to kill my own father. More than make me scorn his honor, my heritage. You made me lose faith in life, justice, truth."

He made a sound, and Crowen was not certain if it was a groan of anger or sigh of regret.

"Cursing you was not enough for me," he continued. "I wanted to punish you myself. Take from you whatever you found precious. Make you suffer, watch you scream. Forever. I did not want to go to the land below. I did not want to rest, or to find my rest in time like the others seem to wish to do. So I stayed above, searching for you, a ghost seeking vengeance on another ghost, hoping the Huntsman would find my restless spirit. I had a use for the Hunt.

"When the Hunt caught me, what I found was better than I could have hoped. The Huntsman was weary of chasing the souls of strangers. He wanted to be free. I told him what I wanted. He saw my pain and hate. We bargained. He traded his task for my youthful soul. His was spent; it twitches within me now, a weak and shriveled thing. But it is enough to sustain me and my desire, as it sustained him and his wish to be free. And nothing else. Nothing. No hope, mercy, or forgiveness. It suits me perfectly."

Tempou leaned back in his saddle and passed the sword blade between his fingers. "The Huntsman rests in the land of the dead. At peace, strong and well with the soul I gave him. He does not care that I've done nothing but hunt for you. You and I are now destined for each other."

"Please," Crowen said, holding out his hands to Tempou, "we have so much to talk about. I owe you, Tempou, and I want to make a just payment."

"What you owe cannot be counted, or repaid."

"But the others, they're willing. They'll forgive my debt in time, Mithete said."

"And I will help them get their satisfaction from you. But I can no more forgive you than myself. I've sacrificed my soul to lead the Hunt. I can never rest, never be satisfied. Your torment with me will never end, Crowen of Fech. Never."

Tempou raised the hood over his head, and his face disappeared behind a veil of darkness. The beasts howled. Rain hissed as it fell through bare branches to land on fallen leaves.

Sharp claws nicked Crowen's ankles and he jumped. Furred shoulders pushed him. Cold snouts jabbed his ribs. Rough armored spines raked his back. A jaw full of teeth clamped down onto his hand and Crowen screamed. The Huntsman rode forward, leaned, and slashed him across the face with the sword.

"Run, Crowen," the Huntsman said. "The Hunt begins."

Crowen fled as a horn sounded. He looked back once, into the burning eyes of a pack of beasts, into the black depths of the Huntsman's hood. Then he ran wildly into a night where no words or music ever break the stillness. ∎

© DONALD W SCHANK

The Cyborg Touch
A. J. Sobczak

The *Explorer* lurched unexpectedly at the jump point exit. I looked across at Michael, slumped forward in his restraints. The concussion had knocked him cold, so it was up to me. I grabbed my set of controls and tried to hold the ship steady, but the violent forces worked too hard against me. I hit the thrusters hard, trying to burst out of hyperspace, but the ship didn't respond, other than shaking even more uncontrollably.

A sudden snapping motion of the ship threw me hard against my restraints. On the monitors, I saw portions of the ship breaking away and small explosions near the main drive. The ship was going to blow, and soon.

I set the controls on automatic, for all the good that would do, and got out of my seat. I grabbed at the release on Michael's restraints, but it had locked up. Another explosion boomed on the monitors, nearer the main drive. I slapped at Michael's face and shook him by the shoulders, hoping to revive him, but it was no good. The booming of the monitors, ever quicker as the ship consumed itself, reminded me that I had to get back and look after the rest of the crew. I leaned over my fiance and kissed him softly on the forehead. Goodbye,

Michael. God be with you.

Debris littered the crawlway to the escape pods. I waited until the last crew member there had gone through. Seven, including Michael, hadn't made it. I started to make my way through, hoping the explosions would hold off long enough.

Even on a nuclear powered jump ship, there are some flammables. Some screwup in design put them alongside the *Explorer*'s crawlway, and I saw flames running along the walls. No one really expected to survive mission disasters; these emergency systems were only for show. I crawled as fast as I could, my palms and knees pounding against the metal floor. The heat seared my back as I crawled, and I became numb to the pain...

I AWOKE with a start, heart pounding, expecting to be in the escape pod. No, that had been three years ago. I felt the same way as then, the same way as I did the hundred times I had relived the disaster in my dreams. My cot was damp with sweat. Relief at being out of danger overwhelmed me, but I couldn't forget Michael's face.

I drew in a long breath. Shipboard routine aboard *Adam Swift* had to go on. I got out of my cot and did my morning routine, wiping myself down quickly with a cool cloth before getting dressed. *Adam Swift* required less work than standard jump ships, but the routine still ruled our lives. Ten minutes after waking, I made my way forward to the control cabin. Barrow would be glad to see me, at the end of the night watch. The watches got awfully lonely with just the two of us running the show. Adam Swift didn't count, not for me, anyway. I still found it creepy to talk to the walls and have them answer back. I couldn't deny the advantages of a cyborg ship, though. Swift never slept and could alert me if a problem ever arose, which it never did.

Sure enough, Barrow was eager for companionship. I couldn't blame him. For almost two years at the Academy, he had been surrounded by other trainees. If he'd made it through that second year and graduated, I'd never have been able to get him to sign on as copilot so cheap. I tried to count my blessings every time his adolescent machismo surfaced. It wasn't easy. Everything was competition with him, especially, it appeared, with women. I played to it a little bit, I admit. I needed my amusement.

"Shoot." I saw that I would lose in four moves. "I concede. Who suggested 3-D chess, anyway?"

"You did, captain," Barrow replied, smiling smugly.

"The boredom must be getting to me, then. I'm not much good at the game," I lied. I didn't want Barrow to develop more of an ego problem, even if the issue was only a chess game. *Adam Swift* was difficult enough to deal with.

"I admit an advantage, captain. 3-D chess is part of strategy training at the Academy. I took the liberty of memorizing the openings with the highest success probabilities."

What an ass. "And I fell right into them."

"Most people do, captain." More smugness. He brushed back his crewcut and threw an arm across the back of his chair. I can't believe that I'd flirted with the idea of him as a lover. That lasted about a day on board, until I got to know him. He might be good looking, but he was no Michael.

Damn him. Why did men have to be like that? "I'll try not to let it happen again, now that I know your secret."

"So you're ready for a rematch?"

"Not today. I've had enough."

"That makes me today's winner. What's the prize?"

Here it comes, macho time. I can enjoy it too. "I didn't realize this was a trophy contest. Fair's fair, I suppose. How about I do the sweeping?" Dust was a constant problem for the ship's electronics, and the ship's robots lacked the precision to do a complete job.

"I had something a little more personal in mind." Barrow's eyes narrowed slightly, just as when he was planning chess strategy.

"Such as?" I batted my eyelashes coquettishly and brushed black curls from my face, knowing Barrow would fall for that. These kids were so predictable. I tugged my uniform sleeve down to cover the pink scar at my wrist.

Barrow swooped in for the kill. "A little kiss, I thought, or a leisurely romantic dinner later. There's nothing much to do for the next two weeks, until we hit port. Captain's discretion."

"In that case," I responded with the sweetness of saccharine, "I grant you half of my watch in Forward Control tonight. And perhaps a cold shower would be in order." The smile dropped right off of Barrow's face. Ah, life is good. Romance with this arrogant kid was the furthest thing from my mind. I wasn't even sure I would keep him on after this cargo run, even if I decided to renew the trial contract with *Adam Swift*.

Barrow packed up the chess set and left for his cabin, tail tucked firmly between his legs. He wasn't much of a shipboard companion. I spent time with him mostly as a favor, knowing how draining the lack of outside contact can be. After twenty years of jump ship experience, I din't have much in common with a kid fresh out of the Academy, one kicked out for insubordination to boot. Talking with Swift was easier. We had more in common, and he was always there—literally—when I needed him.

I went back toward my quarters, pausing at Swift's cabin door. He insisted on the cabin as part of the contract, but why did he want it? Wired into the ship, somewhere deep in its machinery, he had no need for a bunk or storage space. I reached for the handle and almost turned it before continuing down the passageway to my own cabin.

"SWIFT," I asked later as I sat at the control console, "how are the repairs going?" I checked at least once a day. I should have let him keep control during last week's jump instead of overriding.

"Fine. I won't be 100 percent until I have a mechanic work me over with a good set of equipment in dock, but things are shaping up."

"I should have left the controls alone. You knew what you were doing."

"We've been over that, Serina. Any good captain would have done the same thing. It's instinct to take over when there's a problem."

"I can't get over feeling that I hurt you, though. This ship is your body, and I don't want to have caused you pain."

"There isn't anything like 'pain' for a cyborg ship, at least not from bodily damage. I can sense damage, but it's like I'm looking at it, not feeling it."

"Do you feel anything at all? I mean, with no body except the ship . . ." The question was uncomfortable, but curiosity got the better of me. I smoothed my uniform and tucked my right hand up near my left armpit. Swift took a moment to respond.

"I don't feel things in the usual sense, no. All a feeling is," he explained, "is an electrochemical response in the body, triggering a reaction in the brain. Since I still have a brain and electric signals running through it, I can feel things. I simply choose not to, in most cases. The feelings serve no purpose."

"I guess they wouldn't." I rubbed my arms, shuddering slightly at the thought of living without a flesh-and-blood body, not that mine was much to be proud of. The hand went back into the armpit.

"Of course I do have emotional feelings," Adam said defensively. "Those serve a purpose."

"I'm sure they do." I could tell what he was getting at by the tone of his voice. I knew that he saw me as cold and businesslike, and that's the way I wanted him to see me.

"And?" I said, wanting him to finish his thought. Since we'd gotten into this heart-to-heart, or heart-to-circuit anyway, we might as well finish it.

"If you don't mind my saying so, your feelings seem closed off."

Okay, he'd said it. I abandoned the pretense of working at the console. I wished he had a face that I could look at when I talked to him.

"Don't get me wrong, you're friendly enough," he continued. "In fact, I'm growing rather fond of you." That was no surprise. I'd noticed Swift's increased willingness to talk, just to chat rather than with any business in mind. I had reciprocated, and I thought I was friendly enough, but I still felt funny talking to the walls. And I still thought he was an arrogant S.O.B. The way he'd tried to screw me over on the contract terms still rankled. I could just hear him thinking how he would be able to push me around because I'm a woman. The space business has always been like that. Except for Michael.

Swift hadn't let up. "I see you keeping your distance, like you don't want anyone to get too close. I can understand that in my case, but you seem to be putting off poor Barrow."

I laughed. "Poor Barrow? I certainly don't want to encourage his pathetic little attempts at seduction."

"Why?"

"I don't think that's any of your business!"

"Maybe not, and I'm sorry, but you started this conversation."

"Barrow simply does not interest me," I said. That had to be the understatement of the day. "A crewcutted, macho kid like that—maybe the space bunnies in the port lounges go for his type, but not me."

"Why not you? You're an attractive woman, and—"

"Who's talking about me! Barrow's the one with the problem." I hugged my arms around my chest.

"Perhaps," Swift said softly. Softly. I hadn't heard quite that tone of voice from him in the three months we'd been under contract. I wasn't going to break down so easily, though. That's just what he'd like, for me to get all emotional, like a girl. Still, it was easy to talk to him, without a physical presence to get in the way. It was almost like talking to myself.

"What, then?" I asked him. "You think I have a problem? Let's hear about it."

"The *Explorer* accident changed you, Serina, maybe more than you realize."

"So now you're a psychoanalyst? What would you know about the *Exporer*?"

Swift paused. "I've been there too, you know."

He was right. He just hadn't been as lucky as I was when his ship blew. I'd gotten used to him as *Adam Swift*, the jump ship, and had forgotten that he used to be a jump pilot like me.

"I'm sorry, Adam, I didn't mean anything by that, I forgot."

"It's okay. I'd like to forget, myself. I have my accident like you have the *Explorer*."

"Yes, but you ... Well, look at you." I immediately regretted that. He needed reminders no more than I did. I spoke before he did.

"I didn't mean that either."

"I know, Serina. I can guess how you see me. Barrow may not be much of a man in your eyes, but he beats the heck out of what I have to offer." I could tell the chuckle was forced.

"No, Adam, that's not true. I think a lot of you." I realized how true that was after I'd said it. The pause before Swift spoke told me that he wasn't as sure.

"I'd like to believe that, but I still don't think you see me for all that I am. I'd like to show you something. Haven't you ever wondered about my cabin?"

"Well, yes, but I didn't think it proper

to intrude." I blushed, recalling surreptitious attempts to peek inside. Swift must have known, with his eyes and ears all over the ship. How could I have been so stupid, not to mention insensitive?

"Let me show you," he said. "I think you'll be interested."

That piqued my curiosity. I climbed the ladder down to the cabin level. As I neared Swift's door, a remote robot inside opened it for me. If nothing else, he's a gentleman.

Inside the cabin, I marvelled at the array of mechanical toys, electronic parts, and tools. The only clear floor space was a pathway just barely wide enough for the robot. Shelves covered each wall, and each was packed full.

"What is all this?" I asked.

"I enjoy tinkering and exercising my dexterity," Swift replied. To demonstrate, the robot picked up three rubber balls and began juggling. I laughed appreciatively, and the robot took a bow.

"But that's not you," I protested. "That's just a robot."

"He's one of the things I use to express my physical being, just like the controls of the ship. Believe me, it took a long time to adjust my sensations to perform that little trick! Robots don't come off the line with that kind of dexterity."

"I suppose not."

"That kind of performance needs a human brain," Swift explained. "You probably don't realize how rare cyborg machines are, much less cyborg ships. I was the first," he added, pride obvious in his voice, even now arrogant. "I had that swept from as many records as possible. I didn't want to be known as the experimental model."

"I had no idea." I'd read about his accident, but only little blurbs in the shipboard library. It now made sense why the accounts were so brief.

"I was on the team that developed cyborg technology, so when I became . . . available as a test subject, the team went right ahead. We all wanted to be used in the research if the occasion came up. The Mars shuttle accident gave me my chance."

"So you actually helped develop this technology?"

"Yes. I guess I can make that claim to fame."

"So what about the rest of this?" I waved a hand, encompassing the cabin.

"Some of it is just for my amusement." The robot picked up a toy with several ball bearings inside and succeeded in landing each bearing in a small indentation. I clapped enthusiastically, and the robot bowed again.

"Other things are part of my work," Swift continued. "I had to develop finer sensors for the robot to be able to do his tricks and, more important, for work on the ship." The robot touched the end of my sleeve before I could pull away, then rubbed the cloth between its thumb and forefinger. "For example, I can now feel the texture of that fabric. I know what it should feel like, and I've been able to make it feel like that to me."

I noticed some fabric samples on one of the shelves and could understand their significance as both experiments and attempts by Adam to remain literally in touch with his former world.

"What's up here?" I reached up on one shelf and touched a sophisticated headset.

"I wish you wouldn't," Swift asked, just as I pulled the headset down. It was too late. A corner of a framed photograph showed from the back of the shelf.

"Just like you left someone behind, so did I," Swift explained. "That's my girlfriend. I like to look at her once in a while and remember."

"Of course, Adam. I'm sorry. I didn't mean to intrude." I bowed my head, apologetic yet again. I guess sensitivity isn't one of my strong points.

"It's all right. She doesn't know that I'm still alive, and of course she's decades older now. I thought I was protecting her by letting her think I was . . . gone. I was pretty well prepared for the experiment, having worked with it so intensely, but I didn't think she was ready for it. Our staff psychologists agreed that it was better for her to believe that I died."

"How horrible for you."

"Yes," was all he said. It spoke volumes. "I miss her, even after so many years." I detected a catch in his voice, a sob that had never been part of the language synthesizer in the ship's computer.

I pulled my arms around myself. I shuddered just thinking of what that must have been like. Then again, in a way I knew.

"Scary, isn't it?" I finally said.

"In all kinds of ways," he said. "I guess that's why we hide."

"What?" I had no idea what he meant.

"Oh, come on. Those outfits you wear don't fool me. I hide inside this ship, and you hide inside those long-sleeved blouses. What they cover doesn't matter, and you shouldn't use them to try to hide what's really inside."

Wow. That was quite some speech. If it had come from Barrow, I would have slugged him for having the nerve to talk to me like that. Even from Swift, even now, it was hard to take. I counted to ten slowly before speaking. My mother had taught me that much manners.

"I'm not hiding, Swift. I just don't think I offer a very attractive picture, and I don't want to display it." I ran my right thumb along my left sleeve, tracing a scarred ridge.

"I just told you," he said, "it's what's inside that matters, and I think you're hiding that too."

"I am not!" I realized how childish that was as I said it, but it was all I could think of.

"Come on. Remember who you're talking to. I've been there, you know, and I've been dealing with it for a lot longer."

"I suppose you're right. I just have a hard time remembering what it was like before. Even the scars . . . I can't imagine myself without them, but I know other people see them as bizarre."

"And that's why you close yourself off. Like from Barrow."

"Barrow," I laughed. "That twerp. He's seen all he's going to see." Swift laughed too, harder than was necessary. The tension had gotten to both of us.

"No one's even making me the offer," Swift said. The laugh this time was forced. I didn't quite understand what he was getting at, but I laughed along with him.

"We're quite a pair, aren't we?" I said. "So what is this thing, anyway?" I held up the headset.

"That's a dream of mine," Swift said. The robot took the headset from me. "I can talk and feel objects, but it's not the same as being part of your world. I want someone to be able to enter into my world and share it with me. So far all that's been done with this technology is to link one brain, one mind, to a computer. I'm trying to link a second mind."

"Is that possible?"

"I think so, now. The trick is to keep the second mind separate from mine inside the computer, and to be able to allow it to withdraw. If the brain is still ... if it has a body, it also has to stay in touch with that body, to keep it alive. So far I've been successful with letting outside electric patterns in and been able to shut them off."

I thought that over, considering my next step. This new side of Adam was very different, very intriguing. I could see him, amazingly enough, as more of a human being now, not just a cardboard cutout of a macho jump pilot and certainly not just a machine. I mustered my courage.

"Adam ... can I try?"

"Are you sure?" he asked.

"As long as you can get me out, then yes." I thought about the recent accident and how I should have let him keep the controls. I now trusted Swift with my life. Why not trust him with my mind as well?

"Put that on, then." The robot handed my the headset, then cleared a place on the floor for me to sit. "Relax, and follow my instructions. At the slightest problem, I'll pull you out."

I kicked off my shoes and sat against the wall, legs folded under. I put on the headset, not knowing what to expect.

Adam spoke aloud to me, his voice muffled slightly by the headset. "I'm going to connect you with the computer now. I'm getting your feedback, and trying to match your brainwave pattern. I'm locking it in ... there! I've got it!"

I no longer heard him through my ears, but from inside my own head. I thought of how close this was to schizophrenia and shuddered.

"Try not to be afraid," Swift thought at me. "Remember, I can get you out any time you get too uncomfortable."

"I guess so," I said.

"No, think it to me."

I concentrated on my thoughts, trying to strengthen them. "I guess I'm still a little nervous."

"I understand."

I had gotten through! "Oh, Adam, I can't believe we're actually doing this."

"Are you ready to go in deeper?"

"Yes." I felt like I was being led along blindfolded, occasionally getting jolts of color or texture sensations, and sometimes heat and sound. I still saw and experienced the cabin, the cold floor under me, but it was superimposed on the sensations from Adam's mind.

I realized that Adam knew everything I was thinking and feeling, and that scared me. The whole experiment was starting to seem crazy, and I wasn't sure I wanted to continue, to let this man share my innermost thoughts.

"I can understand if this is going a little too quickly," he said. Scary—he responded to my thought barely after I'd had it, much less considered my reaction. "Let me reassure you," he thought to me, "you can get out any time you want. I want you to know how I feel about this, though."

My mind was flooded with warm, tender feelings. I had been experiencing the whole encounter with some amount of scientific detachment, but I realized that I was being drawn in emotionally as well. I was startled at the realization that I was becoming aroused.

"I'm afraid that's partly my fault," Adam admitted.

"How?"

"As you've discovered, I find you quite attractive, and you're feeling that. Barrow's not the only one who thinks you're quite a woman."

I blushed, but I felt my arousal even more keenly. Now some of it was from my side.

"Adam, do you really think so?"

"You can tell."

I could, and I was pleased with the answer. I shut my eyes and shook my head, trying to convince myself that this was really happening.

"It is. Do you want it to?"

I had to answer yes, but hesitantly. Adam, of course, could tell why.

"Bodies don't matter now, Serina, but yours is nothing to be ashamed of. Let me show you."

I stood up. I saw myself undressing slowly, through Adam's eyes. I unzipped my blouse down the front and slipped my right arm out of its sleeve. A band of pinker flesh, puckered slightly, showed at my stomach. I paused, holding the cloth in place.

"It's all right," Adam said. "I know what to expect, and I'm looking forward to it."

I looked down at myself, just as I felt Adam looking at me. Slowly, I uncovered my stomach, revealing the scars. My right hand reached for my left shoulder, and I pulled the blouse from it, sliding the cloth along my arm. I uncovered my arm slowly, tracing a band of scar tissue two to three inches wide from my shoulder to my elbow. Finally, I let the blouse fall to the floor.

"No," Adam reflected my thoughts. "It's not perfect, but it is you."

I could feel Adam's love and lust, knowing both were genuine. I slid my pants down over my hips, pulling my underwear with them. One hip showed a six-inch circle of pink scars. Adam's gaze focused on it, but I knew that it was all right. He was openly curious, but not disapproving. I stepped out of my pants and stood naked. Seeing myself through Adam's mind was like being in front of a mirror, something I had avoided for years. I enjoyed the sensation.

"Lovely," I felt him think.

An image formed in my mind, a tall young man, broad shouldered, with brown wavy hair and blue eyes. His smile was slightly askew, but friendly. His chest had just a few soft curls of hair. I saw that he too was naked.

"Is that ..."

"Me. Or at least it was, many years ago."

"Oh, Adam." Because this was his image of himself, I felt his minor pangs of irritation. He thought his arms were a little too thin and that his stomach wasn't quite flat enough. I didn't see any imperfections.

"Now you know how I feel about you," he said. "You don't like your scars, but they're part of you, part of what makes you special and wonderful."

Michael used to talk to me like that. Adam immediately knew.

"I'm sure he saw in you the same things I see, not just a gorgeous body. People who are really close, really meant for each other, have to go beyond their physical beings."

"That's just how I feel, Adam."

Adam proved his agreement. I was flooded with raw emotion, pure love from him, and creeping in at the edges, Adam's returning desire for me. For me! I found myself aroused again. This time Adam drew me in deeper, and I went willingly, wanting to experience more. Adam clasped me to him and held me tightly in his mental grip. We concentrated on each other, as lovers should, our feelings feeding on each other and reflecting back on themselves. He clearly remembered how it was done, caressing me in all the right places. I thought I was awkward, but I could tell that Adam approved of my light kisses and gentle touch. We stayed together for what seemed like hours, exploring each other and building the sexual power. Physical release came simultaneously, long rolling waves for me and quick bursts for him.

I realized that I was again sitting on the floor, leaning against the wall. I was breathing heavily and my body tingled, covered with a light sheen of sweat. I felt Adam's exhaustion and bliss as fully as my own, and I giggled.

"Now I understand how men feel afterward. You just want to roll over and go to sleep, don't you?"

"Kind of, but with you." The robot, which had been waiting in one corner with its back discreetly turned, now approached me. It extended one arm and softly patted my shoulder. I couldn't help recoiling.

"I'm sorry, Adam, but I'm not ready for that yet. I want to think of you as a person."

"I understand." The robot withdrew to its corner.

"This is already a little much for me." Exhaustion caught up with me. I found a blanket and lay back on the floor curled up under it. I closed my eyes, sensing that Adam was already asleep, but wrapped around my mind. Just like a man. Yes, he was . . . just like a man. Even a little bit like Michael.

I WAS startled into consciousness the next morning.

"Adam, what's wrong?"

"I'm sorry to wake you like that, but it's time for your watch."

"Oh." I really didn't want to hear that.

"I feel the same way. I haven't slept like that in years." I felt his lecherous grin and had to agree.

I reluctantly set the headset aside and dressed, not wanting the previous evening to be over.

As I left Adam's cabin, Barrow came through the passage from Forward Control. He raised one eyebrow in obvious bemusement at my dishevelled appearance. I let him wonder and didn't apologize for being late for my shift. It felt good to take advantage of being captain.

I settled into the captain's seat and quickly checked status. That was silly —Adam would have done all of that. Still, I liked to keep a hand in. I reached for the manual controls, feeling a little playful. I buzzed Barrow on the intercom and told him to strap himself in. Let him wonder about that, too.

I tried a few tentative swings, rolling the ship back and forth, then let loose with a snap roll. I tried more complicated gymnastics as I became more comfortable with the controls. Or were they becoming more comfortable with me? I blushed slightly at the memory of last night.

After half an hour or so, I was done playing.

"Fun, wasn't it?" Adam asked. I realized that he hadn't spoken to me the whole time, but I had known he was there.

"Yes. I haven't had that much fun in a long time."

"Nor I," he said, then paused. "If I may say so, captain, we make a pretty good team. What do you think about renewing our partnership contract?"

"I do," I said without hesitating, then blushed at the slip of tongue. "I mean I will. Whatever." ∎

When the Sun Makes Darkface

by Mary E. Choo

Devot glanced back over his shoulder. The Aunties would be angry if they knew he was here. They didn't want him to look into anything that showed his reflection. Mam must be wondering where he was, too.

He went to the edge of the pond, taking care not to get his feet wet as he leaned over and peered down. The surface, as always, was muddy and rippled. The face that stared back at him twisted and moved with the water, but what he saw of it looked thin and sad, and reminded him more than a little of Jand.

Jand, the only man he could remember, who'd cared and looked out for him. Jand, who'd gone away one day and never come back . . .

Devot felt the familiar tug of loneliness, and he raised his head, looking across to the grieving-trees at the water's far edge. The trees had always interested him, been part of what drew him here, though for some reason he was afraid of them. The leaves grew thickly from the top of their squat trunks, trailing down and showing blood-red stains where the tips met the water. Mam said that the trees would only grow here; they were the Sun's

trees, a part of her anger and sorrow, and that they'd been here since the beginning of her poisoned time. Mam'd told him to remember that, always.

Devot shivered, staring at the knotted, purple roots of the grieving-trees where they wound their way down into the dark water. He blinked, concentrating.

"Something's moving . . . there, just under the water," he whispered. "Just like last time!" Then "Ow-w!" He clapped his hands over his ears as the voices started, harsh, painful . . . he wasn't sure what they said—not words exactly, but he knew they were calling to him from the pond . . . warning him . . .

"Devot!" There was no force in the hand laid on his shoulder, but it felt heavy as stone. He jerked around. "The Aunties told you never to come here again, *never* to go near the water!"

Devot looked at the slim, pale woman beside him. "I had to come, Mam, just to see my reflection—it's interesting—and there's something—"

"They want you," Mam interrupted.

He hesitated, glancing back at the grieving-trees. Then he slipped his hand into hers, letting her pull him back along the woodland path. He'd grown a lot since the last time she'd led him like this, but he hadn't the heart to object. Besides, he wanted so much for her to care.

"If we hurry, we can take the back way, get back before the Aunties notice," Mam said. She looked hot and unhappy in the pale dress and head covering she wore as his caretaker.

Something in her voice made him nervous, and he stumbled several times on the cluttered path, glancing through the trees at the high stone wall at the edge of the woods, wishing he could climb its rough face and run away.

They made their way to the garden at the back of the house. As they passed between the rows of vines and tomato bushes, Mam hesitated and turned to face him, the long green shadows sliding over her face.

"Devot, you will be careful, with the Aunties? You won't argue, this time?"

"That isn't fair, Mam."

"Devot," she was pleading now, in that gentle way of hers. "I don't mean that you have to agree with them —not deep inside—just don't answer back."

She pulled him around the side of the house, crouching behind the hedge until they came to a path. Breathless, Devot forced her to stop. He didn't want to upset her, but his thoughts from the pond still bothered him.

"I . . . I have to know," he faltered.

"What? We must hurry."

"Mam, what happened to Jand? I mean, where did he *really* go?"

The grey light behind her eyes seemed to fade. "I told you—one time, when the Sun made Darkface, the Aunties took him . . . to a place where he could best see and welcome the Sun, answer to her . . . teachings. Then they brought him back here, to finish the ceremony, and he . . . went away."

Her reply, as always, added nothing to what Devot remembered. He'd been left in the house with Last Auntie while Jand was taken away by the others with great fuss and a lot of chanting he didn't understand. And there'd been that feeling, days later, that something was wrong, a deep, sudden stillness inside him—a feeling of losing something, of being afraid . . .

Mam left the shelter of the hedge and crossed the lawn to the front walk, and Devot hurried behind her. He would have lingered in the garden if he could, for he loved the sunlight and trees and all the things that flew and crawled and sang. He'd been afraid all his life of the Aunties and the big dark house with its shuttered windows, frightened too of all the secret fears that came to him in the dark when he couldn't sleep, that were worse when he dreamed. Right now, those fears were there in the daylight, and stronger than ever. And the way Mam was acting . . .

She stopped between the herb borders and turned to him.

"Devot." In the sunlight, her face was smooth and pale, and the smudges under her eyes looked like bruises. "I just want you to know . . . you matter to me." Her voice was soft, and he thought of the warm dark nights when she'd talked him to sleep.

She turned and climbed the stairs, and Devot, confused by what she said, followed. He felt cold, and he thought of the pond and the voices as he and Mam passed under the black shadow of the doorway. They walked a long way through the bleak hallways until they came to the gathering room in the part of the house where the sun never shone. The Aunties liked to meet there, they said, as the absence of sunlight reminded them of their purpose. They were all sitting at the long table, waiting.

Devot and Mam sat down quickly in the two empty chairs at one end. First Auntie faced them from the other, with all the other Aunties crowding the long benches on either side. As they turned to look at Devot, their grey garments made a rustling sound, and there was a faint scent of dried iris.

"You were missed, Devot," First Auntie said. There was a nasty sound in her voice.

"I . . . was off in the grounds, thinking," Devot managed. His hands felt clammy.

"Good," First Auntie said. "It's good you were thinking today." It was hard to see her face in the shadows that slid through the shutters. "Do you know what today is, Devot?"

She knew he didn't. She'd been needling him a lot lately, criticizing. Anger at his fear of her burned inside him, but he remembered what Mam had said, and bit back his answer, shaking his head.

"It's the beginning of your Realization, Devot. You are about to discover your true purpose. Have you been practicing your Devotions?"

"Always," he lied. A mournful cooing of approval from the Aunties echoed in the room.

"Excellent," First Auntie said. "The Ancestors would be pleased." She waved at the many dingy portraits of men that lined either wall.

Devot thought of his reflection in the pond. When he really tried, he could see parts of himself in the portraits—a chin here, something of the eyes, the way the hair grew. He was sure he saw himself in Jand's portrait, with its thin, sad face.

"And now, of course, we must have the meal," First Auntie continued.

"The meal?" Devot echoed.

"The first of your feasts of Realization, Devot." First Auntie leaned forward on her elbows, and Devot could see the muscles of her scrawny neck stretching, the bones moving under the skin of her face. Her eyes were a cold, piercing blue. "You are hungry, I hope, after all that . . . thinking?"

The door creaked behind him. There was a soft padding of feet, and an Auntie placed a large, steaming platter in front of him. He stared at the contents, horrified.

"These will be the source of your Realization," First Auntie said. "We've been including small amounts in your food for some time now, but this is your first substantial taste. They will help you attain your true purpose. No, now control yourself! None of your questions and nonsense!"

Devot took the fork handed to him and poked at the contents of the platter. The twisted grieving-tree roots were hard under his touch. He wasn't supposed to know what they were, that they came from the trees that were part of the Sun's grief; the pond was a forbidden place. First Auntie must know! That's why she was doing this! He remembered how she'd punished him the last time she caught him there.

"It's all right, Devot." Mam broke

the silence, covering for him. "They're only roots, from some place in the woods."

With all eyes on him, Devot struggled with the roots, hacking off a piece. Chewing it wasn't easy; it was tough, the taste bitter and strong.

"All of them, Devot," First Auntie coaxed.

The roots burned in his throat, sinking to the pit of his stomach. As he finished he began to feel clumsy and dizzy, and his belly felt like fire.

"Now," First Auntie said. "Outside, to acnowledge the Falling of the Sun, to make your atonement."

Devot rose unsteadily. Two of the Aunties grasped his arms and lead him through the corridors of leaping shadows. They all gathered on the neat lawn outside, between borders of flowers that were as yellow as the Sun. Devot stared down the path towards the wall; his one attempt to climb it had ended at its top rim of broken glass, and the scars from the cuts seemed to burn from his hands to his elbows. He wished he was one of the nameless visitors who sometimes came through its high gate and was allowed to leave again. His mind was spinning.

"Now, Devotions," First Auntie said. "Remember, Devot, we are responsible to the rest of the world for what you do."

She looked frail and old, but she had a surprising, hidden strength. The blow she gave Devot sent him to his knees. Gasping, filed with the familiar terror, he began.

"I am a son of the sons of the Ancestor." He could see the Aunties, hear their rustling grey gowns as they drew around him, the whine of their long whipping wands as they tested them.

"The First Ancestor poisoned the sky and the Sacred Sun," he continued, sobbing as the blows began to fall on him. "As the blood of his blood, I must share in the blame, atone for his wrongs . . . I must prepare to be called, for the day when the Sun makes Darkface . . ."

Devot dreaded the thought. The Aunties were crooning approval, their faces eager as they whipped him again and again. Only Mam stood to one side with her wand, a set look on her face. He stared at the crimson sunset that tipped the distant wall, his mind filling with thoughts of water and blood, and Jand who had disappeared on that lost, unhappy day . . .

How long could he go on? Devot wondered. How long could he take the beatings, the blame?

And from deep inside himself, from times he couldn't count, came the silent plea for Jand to help him.

DEVOT DREAMED of the roots that night, tangling in his mind, trapping his thoughts. In one dream he saw them through water, and knew he was drowning; something Mam had warned him about long ago when she'd caught him by the pond. And through it all he was aware of the Ancestors and Jand —Jand, laughing in the sunlight on the smooth green lawn, throwing Devot a ball; and Devot, catching it, laughing back and running for Jand's waiting arms . . .

Devot woke to the chill of his bare attic bedroom, the weals on his body stinging. He blinked. A figure stood against the shuttered window, silver in the moonlight that slid through the slits.

"Devot." Mam moved through the shadows towards him, sitting on the plain wooden chair by the bed. "Do you know me?"

"Why wouldn't I?" His throat was so sore he could hardly speak. She touched his hand, and her fingers felt hot, as if from fever.

"You're so cold," she said softly. Then, in a low, bitter voice, "It's the roots." Devot's head cleared a little and he sat up. There were sore spots on his neck and ankles.

"What about the roots, Mam?"

Mam glanced towards the door. She wasn't supposed to be here. The Aunties had never liked her much, and you never knew who was listening.

"Devot, quickly—over to the moonlight. I have something to show you."

Devot struggled out of bed and followed her to the window. As he steadied himself against her thin form, she pulled something from the fold of her robe. Moonlight flashed from its surface.

"A mirror!" he said. Such a forbidden thing! He'd found part of one once, a piece he'd dug up while working in the garden. When First Auntie caught him with it, he'd been badly beaten. "Mam, where did you—?"

She signalled him to be quiet, handing the mirror to him. The moonlight on its surface was very bright, and shone back on him. He saw the reflection from the pond once more, the Jand-face, and as he looked he began to realize something else. Mam glanced at the door again, then pulled a small candle from her robe and lit it, holding it close. He squinted, raising his fingers to his skin to be sure.

"Lines," he said wonderingly. "One or two, and they're small, but . . . that means I'm—

"Old? No, not for a long time yet."

That made sense, Devot thought. He'd heard the others say First Auntie was old. She had a lot of lines.

"Mam . . ." He looked over at her, down into her face. A question fought its way into his mind that fear had pushed aside again and again. "How long have I been taller than you?" Mam's eyes filled with tears.

"Longer than you think, Devot."

As she said this, Devot wondered that he'd never let himself see it before, even in his secret thoughts. One of the Aunties passed a razor over his face every day, and took off tiny bits of hair. Jand had done that to himself, when he'd been here. Jand was older. Devot should have looked past the beatings and the fear that had come every time he'd asked about 'long' and what it really meant. The Aunties explained things or not, as they chose. He should have asked why he was never allowed to use the names for the days and the warm and cold times that he'd overheard from the Aunties, or why they'd never taught him to count as well as they could.

"Why, Mam? Why don't the Aunties want me to know?"

Mam blew out the candle, pinching the wick. "They thought it might make you unhappy, make you start wondering things . . ."

Like how long he'd been in the house, Devot thought, and just why he was beaten for what the Ancestors had done.

"Mam, I know you don't want to tell me, but you must. Just what is this poison that the Ancestor gave to the Sun?" Mam took a deep breath.

"The Ancestor created evil potions that poisoned the air that the Sun breathed, the water She laughed upon, the trees She gave life to and drew strength from in return. In the end everything grew withered and sick, and many things died as a result of the Ancestor's noxious spells, and Sun grew hard and cruel and vengeful . . ." They were the same tired words.

"And now we . . . I . . . must prepare for the time of appeasement, when the world stands still and the Sun blackens her face in grief . . ." Devot whispered. "You aren't really sure what happened, or how, are you Mam? Things aren't spoiled and sick outside now. They're green and alive. Mam, you still haven't told me about the roots, and now there's this new thing, Re-ali-zation—"

Mam hid the mirror and candle in her robe, turning from him. The outlines of her body were hard and pale.

"Devot, there's a reason why I said you should pretend today. Understand that I'll help you all I can—I should have, long ago. You can't escape eating the roots; you should have some anyway, just in case . . ." she paused. "Small portions only," she added. "Watch and wait for my signal . . . I love you, Devot." There was a creaking sound from outside the door. "I have to go," she whispered.

"Mam, wait!" But she was gone. Devot badly wanted her to come back, to comfort him, to explain; about the new word she'd used, 'love,' and what it meant, and all the other things she'd said.

He was filled with new terror. He rolled himself, shivering, into his blanket. He wasn't just taller, he was older. The Aunties didn't want him to know that. They'd beaten him and made him learn about appeasement until they felt certain he'd obey them. In spite of all the arguing and questioning he'd done lately, they'd felt sure he'd never ask about his age, or this Realization they'd mentioned.

There was a creaking sound as his door eased open. Hope stirred in Devot until he saw the two tall, thin figures against the dim light from the stair, smelled the dried iris scent. He lowered his lids.

"I wonder what she said to him?" Second Auntie mused in a faint, dry voice.

"It was a mistake, letting Mam get so close to him, raise him after she bore him. It didn't make for a more compliant subject." Third Auntie said.

"We should never have let her couple with Jand. She was always difficult. I always said letting both of them be with the boy for so long was unwise."

"It's good we have someone ready. And it's such an honour, the way it should be this time, though I'm sure the trees always know when the Sun is pleased, don't mind the wait . . ."

"I never liked using outsiders, even if they were his kin. Of course we had to, especially when it was too far away . . . but the problems with the roots, the travel here after!" Second Auntie sighed. "We must make sure he eats his portion."

"We'll have to be careful though —too much at once can kill him."

"I never trusted Mam," Second Auntie said. The door began to creak shut, stopped.

"You know," she continued, "I heard something today, down by the pond, when I was collecting the roots. There was a splash in the water, a big one, by the far trees . . ." Devot heard Third Auntie murmur some response.

"No, I won't say anything, not until after," Second Auntie rejoined. "The others might think I was just trying to make trouble."

"Still, we'll have to be sure he doesn't sneak off to the pond—everything should be gone, but you never know." After a pause, they closed the door.

Devot wasn't sure what they meant about Mam and Jand, or the rest of it. He worried about what they'd said about the pond, what he'd seen and heard there, but it was more than that. He lay wrapped in his cold and his terror, suspicion and a new certainly growing in his mind.

He was older than he'd dared imagine. He began to see how long it was since Jand left, when Mam said the Sun had made Darkface. Devot had paid for that time with every waking and sleeping breath. And the awful poison his Ancestor had used on the Sun's world, that had once been at the heart of every living thing, might well be gone.

But to the Aunties it didn't matter. Devot knew that now, understood it from everything they'd ever said or done. They only wanted him to take the blame. And in his half-dreaming state Devot's anger rose above his fear of the Aunties and all they'd done to him, and he decided. He'd defy what they'd taught him, whatever it was they were planning. He would watch and listen, and wait for Mam's signal.

And as he drifted into a deeper sleep, he was looking through roots once more, through water, and he felt a deep sadness as the voices from the pond sang softly in his dreams.

DEVOT DIDN'T see Mam during the next days. One seemed to drift into another, and it was hard for him to think, to hold onto his anger. As he recited his lonely words of appeasement, every shadow in every room seemed to blend into one, to weigh him down.

The roots were the worst. He was always alone at the table now. An Auntie would serve him, and the door would be guarded by four others, their whipping wands ready. And every time after the meal, there were secret visits to the bathroom to vomit most of the roots, the worry that he would be found out in spite of the noise of the water he splashed about.

Yet when some of the roots stayed inside him, Devot worried even more. They made him feel cold, and he wondered why Mam wanted him to eat any of them. His throat was still sore, and the spots on his neck and ankles swelled and hurt even more. In his nightmares he felt the roots creeping and pushing through his body, and heard the singing from the pond.

One day the Aunties came for him. He woke to find them crowded in his attic bedroom, staring down at him. Mam was there too, in the background, in her pale dress. Devot felt cold to the core of his bones.

"Come, Devot," First Auntie said. The others cooed and rustled, and he could smell the dead-flower scent of their robes. Mam stood still, with her eyes downcast.

Devot struggled to his feet under First Auntie's ice-blue stare, trying desperately to collect his thoughts. He'd done as Mam said, eaten as little as he could of the roots. There had to be a way out of this, whatever it was. He'd watch and wait for her signal.

They dressed him in a scratchy black tunic and led him solemnly down the long dim corridors and out of the house. He could see the wall in the distance, and his heart filled with longing. He thought once more of the time he'd tried to climb it, and the brief, bright glimpse he'd had of the world beyond.

The procession wound its way down the path and into the woods. The day was sunny, full of birdsong and wood-scents, and Devot's head cleared a little. He found he could manage, in spite of the pain and swelling around his ankles, though he stumbled deliberately to fool the Aunties. After some moments he realized they were headed for the pond, and his heart beat faster.

"Move along Devot. It's time—your day at last," First Auntie said.

"My day?" he rasped. His tongue felt large and awkward, his throat swollen.

"The day the Sun makes Darkface," she said. "We were careless—apparently She'll come earlier than we thought, but no matter. You are blessed to be called. You know what that means? You're lucky, important."

He didn't feel lucky. He felt weak and afraid. The Aunties began cooing and chanting, pushing him as he hung back. He looked around for Mam, but she followed with her eyes downcast. Devot stumbled forward, looking about for somewhere, anywhere to run. There was

nowhere, of course; they'd only find him.

"'I am a son of the sons . . .'" he faltered, darting glances all around as he mumbled hoarsely on, not at all sure what he meant to do. "I must atone for his wrongs . . ." Wrongs that had no meaning, that weren't, any more. So why, why?

He could see Mam's light dress at his left elbow. She hurried him a few paces ahead, and he began to recite as loudly as he could.

"Devot." Mam hissed in a low tone. "You must run—this path, on the left. I found where they hid the ladder—I put it against the wall . . . the glass at the top isn't too bad here. You can climb. I'll slow the others as much as I can."

"Atone, atone in the name of Darkface." The Aunties' cooing chant had taken on a horrible pitch, and Devot took care to stay steps ahead of them.

"Now, Devot!" Mam whirled, taking her wand in both hands and striking the two Aunties just behind, knocking them down. Devot saw the path, ran. His pain and his coarse garment slowed him, but he was still faster than the Aunties. The wall was there, with its ladder and its promise of escape. He started to climb, full of hope, pulling himself up with his arms.

Then the Aunties were shrieking behind him, and pure terror flooded through Devot's body. He grew even colder, and his strength failed. He slipped and fell straight into the Aunties' waiting arms.

The pond-singing started softly in his ears. They dragged him back along the path, then forced him to his feet, pushing and pulling him towards the pond.

Swarming around him with their whipping wands, they chanted and chanted, some stooping to rub soot on their faces. Second and Third Auntie dragged Mam along by the arms. Devot saw she was crying, and the sore patches on his neck and ankles throbbed painfully.

They burst onto the shores of the pond, and the Aunties crowded around Devot, pushing him to the edge of the water.

"Chant, Devot, Chant!" First Auntie's eyes were wild.

"I . . . I am . . ." he couldn't get the words out. Mam was struggling with her captors.

"Never mind! It's happening, in spite of the boy's reluctance." First Auntie raised thin, thankful arms in the air, throwing back her grey-clad head. "She *is* going to do it here, at the pond, as we forsaw! An honour beyond all we could have asked!"

In a heartbeat Devot knew the moment he had always dreaded was here; the Sun was growing darker; she was hiding her face in anger and sorrow. Whatever Realization was, it was about to come. He stepped back, ankle-deep in the water.

"Behold, a son of the Ancestor," First Auntie shrieked above the wild chanting. "We surrender him to you in a manner most befitting appeasement!"

Devot shook his head, dazed. As the moments passed, the Sun's face grew darker and darker. The chanting echoed all around him, as though it were the only sound left in the world.

"No!" Mam broke free. "Stop this! Stop it! Can't you see you're wrong? *Wrong*! Things aren't like they used to be—you don't even know how they were, not really! All you have are a lot of stories, and these terrible ceremonies—you can't do this! You just can't!"

Devot saw the twisted look on her face as she spoke against everything he'd ever thought she believed in. All the lost summers of his life were in her eyes, and he knew how afraid she was for him. Then she looked out over the water, and Devot realized something else; there was something about the pond, something more than the Aunties and the trees and the ceremony, that she'd never told anyone, that she *knew*. The Aunties stopped chanting, and the world grew dim and completely still.

"You're wrong," Mam said again. Then she gave a soft moan and crumpled to the ground as First Auntie struck her with a large, sharp rock, splitting her head open like a melon.

Grief and rage tore through Devot, overcoming his dread. All at once he knew why they beat him. It had little to do with making the Sun happy, or things getting better, at least not any more. It did have everything to do with fear, and two words he'd heard often but never really understood until now, power and hate. Devot saw at last that the Aunties enjoyed all these things. That was the real reason they'd hurt him and Mam; he suspected they knew this, and for Devot this was the worst thing of all.

The chanting began again, loud, cooing. He swung wildly and started from the pond, but something was wrong. A strange, powerful current began pulling at his ankles.

"It's Realization! He feels the hunger of the sacred trees!" the Aunties screeched.

The pond-singing grew louder. It came from deep in the water, each note tingling inside his head. There were words to it now, and he understood them, knew that only he could hear them. He was older, and this was his time, his Realization. Though he had never harmed a thing in his life, he knew what he had to do.

Second and Third Aunties were on the beach, coming towards him with their wands to prevent any further attempt at escape. Devot lunged. He couldn't clear the pond, but he managed to grab both of them, to pull them to him and hold them. All the Aunties began screaming as the current drew him towards the deep end of the pond and the grieving-trees. He felt calm as things twitched and sprouted from his throat, then his ankles, squirming under the water. He held the struggling Aunties fast.

"I'm sorry," he said to them with real regret. He caught sight of his changing reflection in the ripples of the pond. Then the water was up over his mouth, his eyes, and as he sank into its murky depths he saw the Sun's Darkface going away, felt what She felt, and knew She was more sad than angry ...

After some moments, he found he could breathe. Second and Third Auntie were quite still, and he let them drift to the top. He felt sad about what he'd done, though he had no liking for the Aunties themselves. At least they couldn't tell anyone now about what Second Auntie had heard by the pond when she'd gathered the roots. That was all that mattered. He'd done what the root-voices said.

He turned over, breathing from the new, tender shoots that stretched from his neck to the surface of the water. They'd do until he could swim up for air. The pond was clearer here, and he reached down and touched the tendrils on his ankles, looking over to where they joined the roots of the grieving-trees. His heart leapt as the voices in his ears and grew stronger, and one in particular stood out. He looked through the water to see Jand and the Ancestors swimming towards him, all joined as he was to the grieving-tree roots.

There was a confusion of root-voices as they embraced and explanations were made. He saw how Jand and the others could swim up between the grieving-tree roots for snatches of air, to practice breathing the way they once had, the strange things they ate. He also saw how thick their shoots were, and how they'd pulled and twisted at them to weaken them in places.

And Devot understood that he was blessed in his Realization, for all their shoots could be broken soon, and he would lead the Ancestors out of the pond. Thanks to Mam's advice and the Sun coming early, he'd eaten less of the roots. That made his shoots thinner, saved some of his strength.

There was something else, too. Devot thought about the word Mam had used when she'd comforted him in his room, 'love.' He remembered how her voice had sounded then, and when she'd talked of Jand. Mam had loved them both. And he had felt sorry, when the Aunties were drowning.

Still, they should be in for a surprise before the Sun made Darkface again. Devot smiled and rolled over, swimming with Jand and the others towards the roots of the grieving-trees. Then he filled his lungs with air from the long, thin shoots at his throat, and with his new root-voice he began to sing. ∎

Aisha Kydyshia
by David Niall Wilson

The man was obviously a drunk, and his haunted, bloodshot eyes caught Kelly's effortlessly from the end of the bar. Kelly tried to avert his gaze, but it was too late. In a guttural, monotone voice, the man spoke.

"Like stories, boy?" he asked, peeling himself from his stool and shambling closer. His beard, obviously the product of total disregard, was graying and stubbled, shooting out at odd angles. His hair was long, thin and oily, also gray. Coupled with his emaciated frame, tattered clothing, and those eyes, these details joined together to give Kelly the impression of a scarcrow, or a zombie. He immediately began scanning his mind for an escape route.

"Buy me a drink," the man croaked, sliding onto the seat at Kelly's left, "and I'll tell you a story like you ain't never heard."

Something in the way the man spoke checked Kelly's retort, slipping it from the tip of his tongue. He had time, he knew, and he damned sure wasn't going anywhere in the downpour outside. It was battering at the thin wooden walls of the bar with a steady roar, leaking in some around the windows and rolling in waves from the roof of the small patio out front. Besides, this was his last day of liberty in Morocco; he was in no hurry to get back to the ship.

Kelly shrugged, signalling the thin, robed man behind the bar to bring over two beers. The man gave a furtive, distasteful glance at Kelly's new companion, then spun and went for the drinks.

"Name's Barnes," the man said, staring at his clasped, gnarled hands. "Clyde Barnes. Lived here about fifteen years, now."

"You're an American?" Kelly asked, reaching for one of the two beers just arriving. "What keeps you here?"

"Was American," Barnes said, grabbing the other beer tightly. "Now I ain't sure. Been a long time since I was anywhere else."

Barnes turned again, looking Kelly up and down carefully. "You Navy, boy?" he asked finally.

"Yeah," Kelly answered. "In on liberty. We'll be here a couple of days."

"I was Navy, too," Barnes continued, almost as if he hadn't heard Kelly's answer at all. "Did my twenty and headed over here for a little fun . . . some excitement. Have lots of that here, even now that the war's over."

"You're retired?" Kelly asked, surprised. He'd figured the man was a deserter, or some kind of transient. It was a bit close to home to know he faced the product of his own chosen career.

Barnes merely nodded, taking another long gulp from his beer.

"You promised a story," Kelly reminded him, curious now, in spite of his misgivings.

"Started a long time ago," the man began, not looking up. "I heard the story here myself, in this same bar, back in 1952. Morocco was different then . . . calmer. Didn't have all these damned gypsies tuggin' at your arms then, with their hashish and their tapestries. I was in from cruising the Med; we'd been out a couple'a months. Back then we didn't get much liberty . . . not like it is today. We pulled in here to Kenitra, and we was ready for some adventure. We were in for three days, and it was on my last day I found myself here. Had some money left to spend, and I was thirsty. I was half-way into a bottle of that Anisette over there," he pointed at a clear bottle on the shelf behind the bar, "and feeling no pain. That's when I met Raul.

"He was a short man, kind of sad-eyed and quiet, but that night he wanted to talk. Spoke pretty good

English, too. I bought him a beer, don't remember why. Next thing I knew, we was both finishin' the last of that Anisette, and he was tellin' me the story of Aisha Kydyshia."

"Aisha Kydyshia?" Kelly frowned. "What the hell is that?"

The old man's eyes rose again, and Kelly regretted his interruption. "Not a what, boy," the man grated. "Who. Aisha was a Moroccan woman; lived here before either one of us was more'n a parent's dream. She was a princess.

"Seems there was this man, Abdhul Something or other, who was rich and powerful in these parts. It had been arranged since birth that he and Aisha would be married. Weren't a bad deal on either side, to hear the tale. She was a beauty, and he was rich. Marriage never happened, though.

"Apparently this Abdhul wasn't the most reliable fellow. He met up with some dancing girl one day. Up and married her, and left poor Aisha on her own. Of course, 'round here a fella can get away with that kind of thing . . . 'specially if he's rich. She tried to talk to him—her family tried, too. Didn't matter. He'd hitched up with that other girl, and that was that. He was king here, by then, so nobody was gonna tell him nothin'."

"Well," Kelly threw in, signalling the bartender to bring two more beers, "if she was beautiful, it shouldn't have been too bad."

"Ain't like that here," Barnes explained, eyes still fixed on his hands and the beer glass they now held, as though seeking something in the foam or the rising bubbles. "She was shamed by his not marryin' her, and she was young. He didn't give a hoot in hell

about her, but she loved him. He was the king, after all. It was just too much for her."

"What to you mean?" Kelly asked, already thinking he knew what was coming.

"She killed herself," Barnes answered, downing the rest of his beer. "You know the river by the base, the Sebu?"

"I passed it leaving the gate," Kelly nodded.

"She jumped in there. Drowned herself. Way I hear it, ol' Abdhul-whatever-the-hell never even sent flowers."

Barnes grew silent then. Kelly watched him, waiting. Somehow he got the impression that the real story had yet to begin. It was something in the old man's eyes. He waved again at the bartender, this time motioning also at the bottle of Anisette above the bar. Might as well get into the right mood. Hell, the night was shot anyway, with the rain and all, might as well get lit.

Barnes perked up a bit as the small tumbler full of clear liquor slid into his line of sight. The scent of licorice permeated the air. Downing the glass with a practiced toss, the man turned his head quickly, catching Kelly in a stare and holding his gaze.

"Rest of this story you can believe or not. Don't mean a damn thing to me, either way. I saw what I saw, but that comes later."

Chasing the Anisette with a gulp of beer, he went on. "After Aisha threw herself in that river, things started to happen here, weird things. People said that they'd seen her . . . a woman, veiled, walking the streets late at night. It was said that she'd walk up to any young man she saw and beg him to marry her . . . that she'd promise him riches and fame—and love. Only thing was, if you looked real close, you'd see that she had camel's feet, hooves and all. And she was crying, still crying for the love she'd lost."

"No one has taken her up on it, then?" Kelly asked, smiling despite the scowl his expression brought to the old man.

"Ain't a joke, boy," Barnes stated flatly. "Story ain't over yet, neither. Raul, the man I met all those years ago, he saw her. That was why he was here, tellin' his story and drinking himself into a daze. He saw her, and he turned he down. But he was haunted, haunted and lost.

He said she was beautiful. I know, I know, she had camel's feet, for hell's sake, but the look I saw in his eyes told me that he didn't care about that. She must've been somethin'. He was scared, see? He didn't go with her because he'd lived here all his life, and he knew who she was, and then she was gone. It nearly killed him. He waited for her to come back, waited nearly thirty years."

"Where is Raul now?" Kelly asked.

"Dead," was Barnes' answer. "Threw himself in that river down there not a full day after I met him. Drowned. I went down myself to see where it happened. May be coincidence, may not, but I saw tracks there. Camel tracks. Makes a fella wonder a lot of things."

Suddenly very sorry for the man beside him, Kelly asked the question almost as soon as it popped into his mind. "Why are you here?"

The answer wasn't immediate, but it was chilling. "I'm waitin' to meet her, boy. I aim to marry that ghost, camel's feet and all. Aim to have the riches and fame, too. Ain't never had nothin, in my life 'cept enough money to get by on. She can change that. Don't you see?"

Kelly did. He saw a drunken, misled old man with warped dreams and an alcohol fog for a life. He saw loneliness forced to its extremes. He saw more than he cared to, in that moment. The mystery of the man's strange tale was lost now in the stark reality of the man's insanity. Fifteen years in a foreign land, drinking himself into a stupor day-in and day-out, for what? A memory of a deluded friend and a fairy tale.

Kelly couldn't bring himself to speak, so he just let the silence grow until it formed a wall around him. The Anisette was clouding his thoughts with a pleasant, numbing buzz, and Barnes seemed content with the silence, having gotten his pathetic tale off his chest.

About an hour later, when Kelly was working on the last of the bottle of Anisette and dreaming about home, the old man bundled his battered coat about himself and headed out into the night. He did not excuse himself, nor did he say good-bye. The driving rain seemed to part momentarily, then to close again behind him like a curtain. It had the eerie finality of an ending dream, as though the man had never existed. Somehow Kelly was glad. The man depressed him, and he was just managing to crawl back into a more pleasant frame of mind.

It was nearly another hour before Kelly was ready to brave the last moments of the storm and head back to the ship. His thoughts were considerably slowed by the Anisette, and his steps were a bit unsteady as he exited the small bar and walked out into the drizzling rain. It was still warm, so the water was only an annoyance and not that uncomfortable. It cleared his thoughts somewhat, and he found himself wondering about the old sailor, Barnes, and what would become of him.

It was late, and the light of the nearly full moon was limited by the clouds and swirling mists stirred by the warm wind. He did not hurry. The ship was the last place he wanted to be when he was feeling this good. He decided to take the long way back, coming up along the Sebu and through the gate by the massive new power plant the Navy had built for the base.

It was an eerie contrast, the high chain-link fence and the ancient river behind it. He shivered slightly, thinking about the young Moroccan woman, Aisha, casting herself into that river, and the man Raul, who had followed. How many others, all following a fairy tale? He hesitated beneath the awning of the last of the small shops that lined the road leading back to the base. Beyond him was only desolate landscape and the river, separated one from the other by the power plant. He was about to move on when a small movement near the fence caught his eye.

It was difficult, with the mist and the dim light, to be certain, but he thought he saw two figures moving slowly toward the base. One was tall, but stooped. The other was smaller. Something about the scene was odd, though he couldn't say what. Without

considering the wisdom of his thoughts, he followed them, staying far enough away that there was no chance of the sound of his footsteps carrying.

As he neared the base, he realized that he was slowly narrowing the gap between himself and the other two figures. They were becoming clearer, and he gasped in surprise. It was the old man, Barnes, and some woman with long, flowing dark hair. "Poor old guy," he thought. "Must have found him a hooker to fight off the chill."

He stayed back far enough so as not to disturb the two. If the old man wanted companionship of that sort, it was almost certain that he would not want to share it all with Kelly. Besides, Kelly'd had enough of the man and his spooky stories to last a lifetime, and it was getting late. Only a few short hours to sleep before reveille.

He reached the gate a few moments later, and showed his ID card to the Moroccan soldier on duty. The man smiled at him, babbled a few inane words of English, and waved him through. He began the short walk to the pier in good spirits. If it hadn't have been for the clanking sound of a metal gate, he'd have been there in short order.

The sound carried up from his left, and he spun to see what had caused it. The only thing on that side of the road, besides the river, was the power plant. It was lit up eerily by the glare of the moonlight, which was stronger now—as if some of the misting clouds had parted to allow it through. He could see with a strange, surreal clarity, two figures just beyond the fence. There was a gate there, and it was open.

Again his curiosity won out over his common sense. The two figures were the same he'd followed from the town, and they were headed straight for the river. Glancing quickly over his shoulder to be certain he was not followed or observed by the guard at the gate, he crossed the road and slipped through the gate, pushing it gently closed so that it appeared not to have been tampered with. The two he followed had gained a considerable lead, and he hurried to catch up.

All around him were signs of warning and caution in both English and Arabic. The place fairly hummed with energy, standing Kelly's hair on end. He stepped gingerly between the huge transformers and insulators, cursing himself for not ignoring the old man and going to bed.

Ahead, he could see the two much more clearly than before. They were nearly close enough for him to hear what they were saying, and he strained, hoping to do so before they spotted his intrusion. He felt intensely conspicuous, but he'd come too far to turn back now. Besides, he told himself, the two could get in a lot of trouble out here, and he felt that he should warn them.

This in mind, he called out. "Barnes! Barnes, you have to be careful! The voltage is lethal here—stay clear of the insulators!"

The other's shock was evident as he spun on his heels to face Kelly. His eyes shone with anger—and confusion. It was almost as if he'd not been aware of their location until precisely that moment.

The woman had begun to back away as soon as Kelly had spoken, and

was a good ten feet from Barnes before he whirled back to her. "Aisha!" he cried, stumbling forward. "Aisha, wait!"

Kelly watched numbly, the name not lost on him, as the woman backpedaled toward the river. Barnes followed her, arms outstretched, calling her name with each step. It seemed that the woman would back into the very waters of the Sebu, but she did not. She halted several feet from the edge and waited, choosing, it seemed, to ignore Kelly's intrusion. Barnes staggered forward, reaching out to grasp her.

Kelly did not want to avert his eyes, but he knew he had to see. He turned his gaze toward the woman's legs, moving downward with a slow reluctance to fix on her feet. Cloven feet. Impossibly large, hooved feet. The feet of a camel. The feet of a dream. He tried to move forward again then, to stop Barnes, but it was too late.

With a shudder of pent up desire —a moan of deliverance—Barnes encircled the woman's retreating figure with both arms, pulling her tightly to himself as he did so, hugging her until—*the crackle of energy was intense—brutal. The sound was like that of a small streak of lightning. The stench of ozone permeated the air, punctuated by a scream of agonized pain.*

Kelly staggered back. Momentarily blinded by the display of sparks and blue-white light, he nearly fell to his knees, only just missing a lethal fall into one of the huge ceramic insulators. When his vision returned, he retched —heaving the remains of the beer and the Anisette up in spewing fountains.

Barnes—what had been Barnes— was half-erect, arms encircling one of the huge insulators. His frame was withered, blackened. Swirls of brackish smoke still wisped up about him, and a sizzling crackle sounded through the darkness——the crackle of burning flesh. His head was thrown back at a ghastly angle——and his face . . . on his face was the oddest, most chilling expression Kelly had ever seen. It was a smile ——pained and dying, but a smile.

Kelly staggered back out of the power plant gate, turning and running, running for the ship in a drunken, delirious rush. His mind was a blank. His eyes saw nothing. He picked his way through the base by fevered instinct. He clutched the guardrail of the ship's brow and stumbled up——flashing his ID as he crossed, hardly hearing the questions and banter of the quarterdeck watch. He did not stop his forward movement until he finally reached his bunk, where he crawled in ——clothes and all——and passed from consciousness. He would never remember, afterward, if he had slept immediately, or if he'd lain awake, staring in numbed fascination at visions that would not depart his sight. It didn't matter.

THE DAY that followed passed Kelly in a daze. Whatever work he could find to fill his hours, he did it. It wasn't until the ship had passed through the first part of Sea and Anchor detail and was preparing to get underway that he finally wandered out onto the main deck. The sun beat down on him mercilessly, and the entire base was clearly visible from where he stood, perched on the outer edge of the small flight deck. The brow had been pulled aboard, and the Moroccan port-services crew, looking very tiny from his vantage point, were scurrying about, releasing the lines. He turned his gaze away from the furious activity, tracing his route from the night before, tracing it with dread.

There was a group of Moroccan soldiers gathered at the gate to the power plant. Looking more closely, he could see that they were gathered around something——one of the huge insulators. A black, charred looking thing clung to its base——Barnes?

Memory flooded back in, ghost-image memory of moments lost in the blur of a blinding flash. Eyes captured his——beautiful, compelling eyes. Haunting eyes. The ship lurched, peeling itself from the peir as the tug boats latched on. Very slowly, very deliberately, Kelly averted his eyes from the power plant——from the thing that had been Barnes——from those eyes. He could not go ashore. He prayed that, when the Navy no longer pressed his time, he would be able to avoid the haunting challenge——that he would never come back. Laughter floated in the ship's wake, and he felt he could hear footsteps——echoing footsteps. They sounded as though made by hooves . . . ■

A Story from the War
by M. Shayne Bell

I watched Janic walk to the estre-larium. Though he tried to hide it, I could tell his right leg was hurt. Soldiers at other tables looked up from their meals to stare at him. He didn't deserve this, I thought, even if the stares had been because *he* had a discharge and could go home. But the stares weren't just for that. We hadn't met yet, but the roster told me he was my only passenger on the next run out. Already I felt a proprietary interest.

I meant to go to the estrelarium myself, and after my cup of resh'ort tea arrived I went there. The first step into an estrelarium always startles me. With one step a man still walks on a tiled floor, but with the next stars are below his feet. Three steps out he is surrounded by stars. When my eyes adjusted and I could see the faint blue lines that marked the boundary between floor and wall, I walked on. The estrelarium was fairly crowded; I had to walk quite far along the curve of the station before I passed the last group of seated, quiet men and found a place to sit alone, content after an off-ship meal. I positioned my cup on the small table next to my chair and pressed buttons. The blue lines of the furniture disappeared. I sat suspended above a vast gulf of scattered lights.

Then I saw him, again. He stood faintly illuminated in the last corner of the estrelarium, not far from my table. The blue floor lines formed a right angle below his feet and the stars burned around him. He wore the loose, white shirt and khaki pants of a soldier in port, and he stood just under six feet tall with an athlete's build and thick, blonde hair that looked unruly. I wondered what the military did with men like him who had hair no comb could keep in place.

He turned and started to walk slowly away. I stood and introduced myself. "I believe you're Janic Abrams," I said. I offered to shake his hand, but he looked at me uncomprehending—surprised, it see-med, that someone would shake his hand. After an awkward moment, he put up his hand and we shook. "Part of your passage home will be on my ship," I explained.

"I...didn't know, sir."

I punched a button that brought up the lines of a chair across from mine. "Sit down."

He sat down and looked at his hands.

I hoped he would not be like this on our entire trip together. He was my only company on a long voyage. "The military requisitioned my ship and requested my services," I said. Something safe to say. Something to start with. "So I spend my time ferrying supplies from Anara to this station. I was asked to take you back with me to Anara where you can find passage home on one of the civilian lines that still call there."

He said nothing.

"Are you well? Do I need to make special arrangements on my ship?"

"I'm well, sir. Physically."

"Your leg is hurt."

He looked up. "I was bitten, but I've had shots since then to keep it clean."

"Bitten?"

"On Arsat. You haven't read the news'ports."

"No time," I lied. After getting orders to take him on my ship, I'd made it a point to read whatever I could about him, but I thought he might want to talk about it. Sometimes a man needs to talk to another man who doesn't already know the facts. "I just got in," I said, which was true. "But I've heard of the retreat from Arsat. Talk of it fills the channels."

"Did you hear talk of a Captain Morris?"

It was my turn to say nothing. He saw my look, stood, turned his back to me, stared out at the stars. I tried to drink my tea and ended up dumping it and the cup in the table's disposer.

Suddenly he turned back. "The court exonerated him today," he said, "exonera-ted all of us."

He sat back down and looked down. "They would not believe me."

"Believe you?"

"I tried to tell the truth."

I folded my arms. How like the young, I thought. "Can anyone tell the truth?" I asked him. "Are you sure you know it?"

He looked up. "You weren't there."

"No."

"But I was. I saw what happened. It wasn't what some of the others said."

He leaned back and closed his eyes. And thought, evidently, that none of them should have been exonerated. "I'm sorry," I said.

One of the stars above Janic's head began to blink red. The estrelarium grew very quiet. Some of the men stood up. Janic turned around to look.

The star was not part of the retreat, and the Racnor'n had taken it.

I called up the tableside computer. The station had already plotted course changes: losing that star would add a full day to the Anara run. "Damn," I said.

"They had no time to evacuate civilians," Janic said.

I said nothing to that. What could anyone say worth saying about the people left behind? "They've pushed halfway to Earth," I said.

The star quit blinking but remained a solid, Racnor'n red. I stood to go. "We leave as soon as my ship's loaded," I told him.

He stood up till I had walked away, as if I were a military officer.

WE LEFT the station the next afternoon at 1300 hours. Janic came aboard well before then and helped with the loading. I was glad for his help. But he kept to himself after that, for two days.

On the third day, however, he told me his story.

I found him in the ship's lounge studying a schematic of a naked Racnor'n on the library screen.

"The drawing's wrong," he said. "The snout tends to be longer, and the arms are heavily muscled, strong. Their fur isn't just brown—it can be speckled with white and grey."

I sat down. "It's an old article," I said. "From before the war."

"From before we knew about tryptophan."

I nodded. Human tryptophan causes a mild euphoria in the Racnor'n—an addictive euphoria. Janic and I were quiet then, for a time, busy with our own thoughts, and I was either tired or preoccupied because I became aware only gradually that Janic was talking again, to me, about what had happened to him.

"The marsh was steaming," he said. "The temperature had suddenly dropped to somewhere between twenty and thirty degrees below zero. The open water seemed to boil in the cold, sending up a steam through which we could see nothing clearly.

"And we were hungry because we were put on one-quarter rations and could get no more food till off-world. Our officers sent us out in groups of three to patrol both sides of the road we kept open for troops retreating from the steppes —troops that never came. It grew dark. I was testing the depth of a pond of steaming water to see if Eran, Branc, and I could walk through it or if we had to find a way around when Eran touched my shoulder. 'Janic—up!' she whispered.

"I looked up. A thousand blue lights, it seemed, were drifting down through the mist, twisting around the branches of trees silhouetted in the dusk, falling slowly,

slowly to the ground.

"Someone started shooting. Eran and Branc ran into the brush by the pond. Only then could I break away from the sight. Eran had tripped and lost her cap. I found it in the snow and gave it back to her, then saw Racnor'n all around us in the mist. I heard shooting and screams. I looked up and saw a Racnor'n floating just above me, struggling to slash my eyes with its knife. I fell on my back and shot it from the ground. It twisted in the air and slumped down next to me. The blue light on its belt blinked out.

"Branc fell across my legs and did not move. I sat up and pushed him off. 'Behind you!' Eran shouted. She shot something dark in the brush behind me that fell and knocked snow in my face.

"Then Eran fell. I shot a Racnor'n in the tree above her, but three of them jumped on my back and jerked the gun from my hands. They took Eran's and Branc's guns and motioned for me to get up. I helped Eran up. She wasn't hurt —they'd just knocked her down. We held onto each other. The tallest Racnor'n came only to my chest, but they had guns and knives. We did not try anything.

"The shooting around us stopped, though I still heard screams. The Racnor'n made a stretcher for Branc's body and motioned for Eran and me to carry it to the west, away from the road, but before we could start one of the Racnor'n tore the wraps from his snout and bit off most of Branc's left cheek before the others knocked him down.

"I stared at the Racnor'n's teeth. I had seen Racnor'n teeth in the skulls displayed at base camp. I had seen them in the mouths of the Racnor'n we killed. But I had never seen them alive: sharp and wet. The Racnor'n stood up and sullenly rewrapped his snout.

"I took the back of the stretcher so Eran wouldn't have to look at Branc, and we carried it far into the night. For a time, we could hear screams behind us from the direction of the road. About a third of our company came up around us, all of them bearing stretchers with human bodies. The Racnor'n left their own dead in the marsh.

"They made us climb a ridge where they had dug one of their bases. Hundreds of Racnor'n waited inside. When we walked in, they wailed in greeting. The wailing echoed around us. A lot of them came and took the bodies somewhere, but the Racnor'n soldiers who had captured us made us walk in single file down a series of corridors so low I had to walk hunched over. Eran walked in front of me. The corridor finally opened into a large, round gallery. They chained us to the walls. I thought at first that the room would be our prison. The Racnor'n soldiers who fought us in the marsh crowded inside, wailing. They struggled, it seemed, to stand close to a flat altar of sorts that stood in the center of the gallery, and they tore off their white, one-piece winter uniforms and threw them on the floor.

"After all of us were chained to the wall, an old Racnor'n walked in. He was fat, and the fur had fallen from most of his belly. He made his way to the altar, turned, and pointed back at Eran. The room grew suddenly silent. They stripped her, took her to the altar, tied her across it."

Janic ran his fingers through his hair and looked away. I got up to check instruments that needed no checking, to give him time to collect his thoughts and decide whether he wanted to go on or not.

"They swarmed over her all at once," he began when I sat back down. "She screamed twice. They were eating her."

He stopped again. "I thought I was next," he said finally, "but they took someone else. I did not hear his screams. I heard only Eran's screams the rest of that night. By dawn the Racnor'n were glutted. A few of them dragged the nine of us left down a series of stairs to the depths of their base where cold water dripped from the ceilings. They shoved us into nine separate, tiny cells that had pools of water on the floors. The walls were wet. I had to crouch on my heels because the ceiling was so low. The doors had no grates——we could not talk. There were no lights."

A Class A alert came through on the ship's comm just then and interrupted Janic's story. I punched it in where we sat, and we listened to it. It warned all civilian craft of a Racnor'n thrust into areas I planned to pass through on our way to Anara, so I hurried to the cockpit to plot course changes.

Janic came in just as I finished. "Is it all right?" he asked.

It was as "all right" as it could be. We talked in there after that so I could watch the ship's scanners more closely. As I listened to Janic, however, I realized that his story of battles and aliens merely covered the surface of what had hurt him. Something deeper, something more painful had touched him in the dark below the surface of a lost world.

"My legs went numb," he said. "I tried to lean against the door, but I slipped and fell into the water. After I got wet, I just sat, waiting in a corner by the door. I knew they would come for me, sooner or later, and I resolved to die fighting them.

"I don't know how much time passed. I had even quit shivering when I saw a light shine on the water under my door. That roused me. I crouched back. I heard a key in the lock. The door slammed open. But the light was bright and, somehow, faced with a Racnor'n, I could not make myself move.

"I had not expected food. The Racnor'n stood in the doorway, a gun in one hand, a bowl of steaming mash in the other. Something golden and braided dangled from his belt. All at once I realized it was a woman's scalp. Seeing that was enough.

"I took the bowl and threw it in the Racnor'n's face. He staggered back and shot his gun. The charge burned past my left ear. I knocked the Racnor'n down and dove out of the cell. Flashes of gun light burst around me from behind a cart with lights on its sides and bowls of mash on top of it. I lunged for the cart and shoved it back against the Racnor'n guard. His shots went wild and hit the ceiling with a burst of red sparks. His gun clattered to the floor. I heard the first Racnor'n struggling to get up behind me. I rolled back against him, knocked him down, tore the gun from his hands, and shot him.

"The lights on the cart blinked off. I could see nothing in the sudden dark. I was breathing hard, and I was afraid the other guard would hear me and shoot. I did not dare move for the same reason, so I sat waiting, listening. I heard only water dripping in the pools of the corridor.

"All at once the Racnor'n crawled on top of me and bit my right leg again and again. I clubbed him with the gun, but he managed to bite my stomach twice before I could throw him off and shoot him.

"I crawled to the cart and turned on the light. Both Racnor'n lay dead in the corridor. Blood dripped from the mouth of the one who had bitten me, and I realized the blood was my own because it was red.

"I stumbled to the first Racnor'n and searched his clothes for the keys. He carried only one. It unlocked the cell door next to mine, but my hands were shaking so much I dropped the key. The man who rushed out looked at me, picked up the key before I could reach it, unlocked the next door, gave the key to the man in that room, and came back to help me bind my wounds and stop the bleeding. He tore off his own shirt and ripped it into strips which he wrapped around my stomach.

"I knew him well. He was from my home planet. Just before the retreat he had been assigned to my company as a specialist on Racnor'n bases. We were good friends. His name was Nathan.

"'I didn't know you were still alive,' Nathan whispered to me.

"The others all stood around, shivering, wet like me. Some were crying softly. Captain Morris picked up the guns, kept one for himself, handed the other to my friend. 'Get up and lead us out!' he hissed. 'You've studied these bases.'

"Nathan tried to finish tying up my leg.

"'Get up!'

"Nathan stood up. I finished bandaging my leg.

"'This is a Type C base,' Nathan said. 'But even so, we can't just walk out of it—and they'll come looking for these Racnor'n.' He paused. 'Can someone here fly any kind of ship?'

"A girl next to me raised her hand. 'I can fly our own land-ships, and I've seen a demonstration of Racnor'n instrument panels.'

"'You'll do,' Nathan said. He grabbed the girl's arm. 'I'm a pilot, too. Stay away from me. If one of us gets killed, the other can still fly the rest out.'

"'Just a *minute*.' Captain Morris shoved the girl back. 'I'll give the orders here.'

"The rest of us just looked at him, quiet.

"'We'd never get through the exits,' Nathan explained, all at once. 'But we might steal a ship. That's what I recommend, Captain.'

"'Do it,' Morris said.

"While the rest closed and locked the doors to the cells, Nathan found the hand-light the guard carried. He and some of the others dragged the two Racnor'n into the last cell, pushed the cart in after them, turned off its lights and locked the door. We set off.

"Nathan led the way with his light. Captain Morris and I brought up the rear. I could not keep up. I had lost a lot of blood, and the leg the Racnor'n bit grew stiff and numb—something I expected, of course; a Racnor'n bite can paralyze any mammal's limbs. After a time, Captain Morris simply left me behind without saying a word. Nathan looked back, saw what was happening, and made one man stay behind to help me keep up.

"The stairs to the next level were guarded: two Racnor'n sentries stood in a square of light at the top with their backs to us. The entrances to the flight deck were just down the hall from the sentries. Captain Morris and Nathan crept to the stairs, took careful aim, and shot them. One fell immediately. The other turned and slumped into an alarm panel. A thin, piercing wail filled the darkness.

"We bolted up the stairs—at least, the others did. Nathan came back for me and dragged me after the rest. We met where the corridors branched.

"'Leave him!' Captain Morris hissed.

"'Yes, leave me—with a gun,' I gasped as I slumped back against the wall. 'I'll keep them off as long as I can, give you more time.'

"Nathan spat on the floor. 'If this base is standard Type C, both tunnels lead to flight deck entrances. Take the left and turn right at each branch of the corridor; take the right and keep turning left.'

"Which meant he was not taking orders: he wasn't going to leave me. Captain Morris looked angry enough, then, to kill him.

"Racnor'n wailed somewhere behind us.

"'Two groups have a better chance than one.' Nathan said. 'Split up and run.'

"Captain Morris shoved the female pilot to the left. Four others followed them. Nathan pulled my arm around his neck and ran with me to the right. Lerah Bally, a friend of Eran's, pulled my other arm around her neck and ran with us.

"A shot of light from a Racnor'n pistol slammed into the rock wall ahead of us. The corridor ahead branched right and left; we turned left. We could hear Racnor'n wails behind us.

"'Turn right,' Nathan hissed at the next branch. We turned right down a narrow corridor with no lights. A Racnor'n troop rushed past in the lighted corridor. Ours branched. We turned left. Once around the corner, Nathan turned on his hand-light. 'This route will take longer,' he explained, 'but it will still lead to the flight deck through a service entrance.'

"We rushed along the tunnel turning left each time it forked, all of us hunched over because the ceiling was so low. Suddenly Lerah tore away from me. 'I heard something behind us,' she whispered.

"Nathan shoved me up against a wall, turned off his light, drew his gun. 'I'll fire at the first flash and then both of you run,' he whispered.

"We did hear an ominous sound out of the dark—a tapping on the rock floor of the corridor: one, two, sometimes three times in a row. Something hit my cheek and ran down to my mouth. 'Water!' I gasped. I realized later that the flight deck

temperature would be kept higher; the ground around it would thaw. We heard dripping water in the corridor.

"'Let's go,' Nathan said. 'We're almost there.'

"We ran again.

"'I heard something more,' Lerah insisted, 'not just the water.'

"But ahead, around the last left fork of the tunnel, Nathan's light reflected off a metal door. 'The flight deck's through there!' Nathan said.

"A bolt of light shot between Lerah's head and mine and struck the door. Nathan threw down his light and dropped back. 'Keep running!' he shouted, while he fired behind us.

"Lerah and I were at the door. Lerah fumbled with the handle and opened the door, and we stumbled into the glaring light of the flight deck. Nathan plunged through after us, slamm the door shut and bolted it. Shafts of light struck the walls around us. We dove for cover behind crates of Racnor'n bayonets.

"Four ships stood ready on the deck, their noses pointed at gaping holes in the cave's ceiling. The door of the nearest ship stood open. Through cracks between the crates we saw the female pilot, Captain Morris, and only three other men run up the steps to the ship. Captain Morris was firing madly.

"'Go!' Nathan yelled. He rolled out into the open, firing at the positions of Racnor'n sentries. Lerah pulled my arm around her neck, and we ran. I fell twice. The second time, Lerah screamed.

"I looked up to see Captain Morris hit the face of the pilot. Both of them disappeared inside the ship. 'He was trying to close the hatch,' Lerah gasped. 'But she stopped him.'

"Lerah helped me up. We ran, afraid of

being left, gained the stairs, and fell through the hatch. The others stood inside clutching the handholds that serve for seats in Racnor'n ships. Lerah tore the belt from her pants and tied my left arm to one of the handholds while we watched Nathan fall back.

"The service door Nathan had barred glowed bright red; it finally blew apart. A horde of Racnor'n poured through, wailing madly. Nathan turned and ran for the ship. Captain Morris looked out, saw the Racnor'n soldiers and closed the hatch.

"'Take off,' he ordered.

"'Let him in!' I shouted.

"The girl at the controls did nothing; she just stared. Her mouth was bloody where the captain had struck her.

"I struggled up, reaching for the hatch controls, but the captain kicked me back. 'Take off, or they'll kill us all,' he said.

"The girl turned to her controls. Something hit the door once. We lifted up and spiraled out into a clear night sky blazing with stars."

THE PORT screens of my ship blazed with stars. Janic stared at them. I kept the easy wartime platitudes to myself. Janic was beyond believing them, beyond needing them.

"And they exonerated us," Janic said, finally.

"Why shouldn't *you* have been exonerated?" I asked. I could see no reason for other action.

"I should have insisted that they leave me—delayed until they had no choice but to run without me. I slowed them all down—slowed Nathan down."

"Could Nathan have dealt any better with leaving you?"

Janic looked out of the port for a time. "We shouldn't have left him, that's all," he said, finally. "People should never leave each other."

WE REACHED Anara three days later, never having encountered a Racnor'n cruiser, though other ships behind us had trouble. I tried to get Janic to stay on with me. I needed help with the ship. Help was nearly impossible to get during the war, but he insisted on going home so he could convince his family to move deeper into human territory. I watched him walk away, alone, through the crowded docks.

But I was not through with Janic. Two years later, I met him again. I stood surprised to see him in an officer's uniform. He had reenlisted when the war eventually threatened his home world. At the time I saw him, he and his men had just returned from the operation that took back the planet where he had been captured; in fact, he led the attack on the very marsh base where he had been a prisoner. The Racnor'n kept it operating, though in that planet's summer each level probably became a watery bog.

"To take it, one of the first things we did was knock out their pumps," he explained.

When we sat down in the station's estrelarium he grew serious. We talked of the past. I wanted to know what he had found. "There was no sign of him," he said. "I found nothing left from anyone of my company—not a ring, a shoe, a pair of glasses. Nothing."

He told me before he left that he often dreamed of Nathan—a Nathan still running in dark tunnels, still alive, and hungry, cold, wet. I have dreamt of him too, dreamt dreams of horrors not always alien. At such times, when I sit up in the night, I see only the dark between the stars. ∎

Not Another Unicorn
by Mary Soon Lee

The weeks leading up to the Midsummer Festival were always busy, but this year was the worst that Henna could remember. From daybreak to dusk she measured and stirred, sliced and crushed and poured the ingredients for her concoctions. Her thin middle-aged face was pulled into an unaccustomed scowl, her hazel plaits bouncing angrily against her back. For, however vigorously she sieved and cut and weighed, her mind kept returning to the Princess Carina.

"Spoiled minx," Henna muttered to herself on Midsummer Eve. She tipped a tincture of pansies into the hissing cauldron. "Didn't even bother to ask me before she went to that pompous old fool. He may have a certificate from the Thaumaturgical College, but he can't create so much as a rabbit without help."

Her nose wrinkled as a faint odor of rotting vegetation wafted upward from the cauldron. She snatched the jar of cinnamon and tossed a handful into the boiling brew. With luck, there should be enough to fashion the last few leopards. Just as well, if she had to shape another cat, she'd scream. Over the past four days, she had made small leopards, blue leopards, leopards with three tails, and others with six feet. Fully half the ladies of the court had flounced into her shop, equipped with too much money and too little imagination, and demanded a leopard.

That was also the princess's fault.

Last year, when Princess Carina still deigned to call at Henna's, she had ordered a two-headed purple leopard for the midsummer celebrations. The animal had been one of Henna's finest creations. Its eyes glowed in the dark, flecked with silver dust, its coat shimmered from indigo through to deepest violet, and it maintained its shape for a full month before starting to dissolve.

Henna sighed. Giving that magnificent beast to the princess had rankled even then. But Carina was as malicious as she was vain, and Henna had no desire to discover precisely how dank and gloomy the palace dungeons really were.

The doorbell jangled noisily.

"Go away!" shouted Henna. "Can't you read the sign? I'm closed until after the Midsummer Festival."

"Of course I can read the sign, though your lettering is clumsier than a child's. I need to speak with you immediately."

"How unfortunate for you. I'm

busy." Henna picked up her pestle and ground away at some herbs. The plants disintegrated to a green smear as her arm worked harder and harder. She would recognize that smug, aristocratic drawl anywhere: the Magus Bartholomus with his prized doctorate.

"Open the door, woman, or I shall——"

"Or you'll what? Spell open the lock? The last time you tried an opening incantation, your robes unbuttoned in the marketplace." she grinned at the magician's indignant snort.

"Open the door——" Bartholomus's staff rapped sharply against the cobblestones, "——or I shall kindle the thatched roof over you miserable head."

"You wouldn't dare, old man. One deed like that, and the guild of sorcerers would have you killed. No destructive magics, isn't that right?" Henna's voice was steady, but her fingers trembled against the pestle. Bartholomus's sole aptitude as a magus was in working fire. If she angered him, he might risk igniting her shop.

"My . . . apologies, lady. I forgot my manners in my haste to confer with you. Kindly permit me inside, and I shall reimburse you amply for your patience."

Henna blinked. Bartholomus's reluctance to humble himself seeped into his tone, but there was something more than that, an undercurrent of genuine fear. For a moment, she caught herself feeling sorry for the old man. Mostly, he was harmless enough, fussing over his tiny garden with its azaleas and fuchsia and a single magnolia tree. Well, if he could be civil, then so could she. She wiped her hands dry, and opened the door.

Bartholomus stepped inside, a short round-faced man, his bald head emerging incongruously from the splendor of his scarlet robes. His eyes widened as he stared at Henna.

She followed his gaze down her stained tunic, blotched with a hundred shades of dye. "I haven't had time to keep washing and cleaning. What can I do for you?"

"It's the Princess Carina. As you may have heard, she visited me recently concerning a possible commission."

"I heard."

He had the grace to look uncomfortable. "Yes, indeed. I assure you that I attempted to dissuade the princess, but she is a very forthright young woman. She told me that if the beast wasn't ready by Midsummer, she . . ." He tugged at the collar of his robe. "Maybe it's best if I omit her phrasing. Suffice it to say that she threatened me in terms unbecoming to her station. Regrettably, I believe she meant every word. and so I am in something of a predicament."

The man's round face and his bald pate had turned quite pink. He was rubbing away at the corner of his robe as though determined to wear through the satin.

Henna pushed a stool toward him. "Here, take a seat. Now then, what exactly is the problem?"

"The princess requires a unicorn by tomorrow morning."

Henna almost laughed out loud. Not another unicorn; sooner or later, every noble lady came down to Henna's and requested a unicorn. Even the poor flabby Countess of Arques, who couldn't have charmed a hamster, had arrived early one morning, face flushed, and stammered that she wanted one of these mythical creatures. Henna had given the countess a miniature phantasm, complete with gleaming horn. At least the countess had been a true virgin, many of the ladies were spurned even by the phantasms.

But she bit down on her lip to swallow the laugh. For Bartholomus was gazing at her in desperation, his knuckles white against his collar. Sternly, she remembered his snide remarks in the past, the evening she'd spent crying after they first met, back when she was too young to know better.

"So you want me to shape a unicorn for you," she said finally, without a trace of gentleness. "And maybe I will, maybe I won't. My fees would be——"

"No, no, you don't understand. Princess Carina insists upon a real unicorn, not a phantasm. Otherwise, she will have me hung, drawn and quartered, and she will thread my finger bones into her next corset."

"I didn't think there *were* any more unicorns."

"Precisely."

"Then why didn't you just tell the princess——"

"I tried! She's listened to too many minstrels singing their romantic nonsense."

"I'd heard she'd done more than *listen* to the minstrels," murmured Henna.

"Quiet!" Bartholomus stood and paced across the floor, his staff tapping out a staccato rhythm. "I cannot afford any further delay. You must simply follow my instructions. Together we will attempt to create a unicorn solid enough to satisfy the princess. If we succeed, I will reward you handsomely.

Now, fetch me an oil lamp."

Henna didn't move an inch. "Let's get one thing clear from the start, Bartholomus. *If* I agree to help you, you will stop treating me like a lower life form. You will not sneer at me, or order me around, or——"

"Agreed, woman."

"My name is Henna."

"Henna, then." He pulled a gold-embossed book from a pocket, and flipped it open. "Spells of the coarser emotions, of illusion. Ah, here it is, spells of true formation."

Henna leaned forward, her eyes intent on the thin sheets of paper that the magus handled so carelessly. She had never dreamt that the magi laid down their knowledge in books, so that one could simply read it. For there was no doubt, the spells were not even encoded. Her mouth was dry as dust.

"Let me," she whispered, "let me hold that for a moment."

Bartholomus gave it to her, his pale eyebrows arching, the barest hint of a smile curving his lips.

She touched the creamy smoothness of the pages, the scent of leather floating from the cover. All those secrets in this slim volume, far more than she had ever pieced together from hearsay and village witches.

"I propose a trade," said Bartholomus, and she saw in his eyes that he had planned this from the start. "That book in return for your help this night."

Henna hesitated. Already, she suspected that the ink would fade from the pages by morning, that the book was baited with a thousand traps. But surely he wouldn't risk her ill will before the unicorn was fully spelled. For every spare second until then, she could memorize the incantations.

The magus's smile broadened. "Well, Henna?"

Slowly, she nodded. "Agreed."

"I need a more binding oath than that: swear it."

Henna glared at him, but said, "By my father's name, I swear that in exchange for this book, I will help you tonight."

BY THREE o'clock in the morning, Henna was exhausted. Errant strands of hair had worked free of her plaits and straggled damply across her cheeks. She stared down at the spell she was stuck on: The Creation of Small Beasts of Field and Wood. Or in one word, a mouse. She had been working for hours, her neck was cramping, and she hadn't even managed to make a mouse.

"Discipline, that's what you lack, woman," said Bartholomus. "Can't you concentrate for once in your life?"

"I'm trying! If you think you can do any better, go right ahead."

"Temper, temper." Using a handkerchief, he delicately nudged at a scrap of gray fur lying on the bench.

Henna reached past him, her lips pressed tight. She picked up the furry lump and dropped it into the crate with the rest of her failures. How that man could compress so much disdain into a few syllables was beyond her. Without looking at him, she laid out five gold beads at the points of a pentacle, arranged the leaves and corn in the center. Scowling, she focused her mind on mice, little white domesticated rodents with twitchy noses, the alarming hop of the wild mouse she had caught as a child. "Mus, mus—"

The five gold beads in front of her wavered, dissolved. In their place squeaked an oversized mouse, as large as a cat. Its fur was an uneven patchwork of pale brown and white and sickly orange.

Henna blinked. "Hey, not bad though I say so myself. What do you think, Bartholomus?"

"Interesting. I think it's very interesting how much better you fared when you were angry."

"It's only a question of practice. I'll try that once more." She smoothed open the book.

"No." A shadow fell across the paper. Bartholomus reached down and flipped the page over, and over again, and again. He tapped the book with his index finger. "Here. The Creation of Magical Beasts, Part the Third, The Unicorn."

"What are you doing? I need more practice—"

"Evidently." He glanced at the giant mouse, which was nibbling away at one of Henna's early mistakes. "But I don't have sufficient gold to indulge you. So the only remaining variable is the strength of your motivation."

Henna looked at him properly for the first time in hours. A deep furrow creased his forehead, aging him by a decade. "Just how much gold is left?"

"Enough for a single attempt at this spell." He placed twelve gold beads on the table, his eyes hard as weapon metal. "And if you don't succeed, I shall burn you and your shop to the ground. It will afford me no pleasure, yet nonetheless I swear this by my father's name."

Past caring, Henna ignored the odd hoarseness of his voice. "*Get out* before I break your bald head over this bench."

"How foolish of me. I was sure you'd sworn on your father's name that you would help me this night."

Almost, Henna reached to throttle him, and yet did not, trapped by her own oath. "Very well, old man. I'll try your spell. But if you so much as whisper one word of a fire chant, I will——"

"You will burn," he said softly. "If I say it, have no doubt that you will burn." He glanced down at the book. "Let's proceed, shall we? Two measures of mercury . . ."

"Shut up," Henna said tightly. "And get out of my way."

Blood beat against her temples as she brushed his arm aside and read through the spell a single time. In silence, without another look at the book, without a glance at the old man, she poured five liquids into five flasks, drew a twelve-pointed star on the dusty ground, and placed the gold beads at its points.

"Unicornis." She raised her arms, picturing the silvered mane of a matchless horse, the gold richness of a lion's tail. The flicker of a candle caught her eye, and for an instant she wondered what texture the horn would have. "Unicornis!"

White light shimmered between her palms, coalesced into a beast the color of moonlight, scented of April dew. But the top of its head barely reached Henna's knees, and it had *two* horns. A bicorn, not a unicorn.

"What?" Henna blinked in dismay. True, the worth of an animal wasn't determined by its height, and both horns were the epitome of grace. Yet she knew that would do nothing to mollify the Princess Carina.

From behind her, she heard a curious gulping sound: Bartholomus. Belatedly, she remembered his threat. Visions of the walls about to leap into flame brought her swinging round.

The magus wasn't chanting, he was crying, the arrogant lines of his face crumpled. With both hands he tugged at his collar.

Yet however miserable he looked, he had done nothing to deserve her sympathy. "What's wrong, Bartholomus? All talk and no fire?"

"I never intended to hurt you," he whispered. "What good would that do me? It's too late now."

Henna snorted. "You were quick enough to threaten me. You swore by your father's name——"

"My *father?*" His chin rose. "Woman, I've cursed my father every way I know how. But for his pride, I would never have graduated." He faltered, his voice quavering again. "And I would never have been in this predicament."

Henna opened her mouth to tell him that it served him right. But he looked so forlorn, that she couldn't bring herself to do so. "Bartholomus, why don't you leave town for awhile? If you set off now, you can be miles away before the princess wakes."

"I'm too old for running and hiding." He stared at her sadly. "Keep the book, Henna. I'm going home." Leaning heavily on his staff, he walked out into the night."

Absurdly, as the door closed behind him, Henna felt a twinge of guilt. If she had only concentrated, the spell might have succeeded. No, that was nonsense, she owed the man nothing. And still . . . She lifted the book, and slowly began to read.

"USELESS!" HENNA threw the book down. She had read it from cover to cover, and she was no closer to a solution. Spells of enlargement, potions to cure or cause disease, incantations to transfer the souls of the dying into fish or plant or beast—none of them were any use. If she was caught working any of the destructive magics, the guild of sorcerers would ensure that she was killed.

Not that she even had the gold to attempt such a spell.

She paced across the room, past the oversized mouse, past the bicorn, its two horns resplendent in the sunlight. *Sunlight*—she must be nearly out of time. Grabbing the book again, she flipped through the pages as she walked to and fro: Illusion, Enhancement, Exchange. She passed the mouse again, and stared at it thoughtfully.

Ten minutes later, she was running barefoot through the town, the sun-burnished cobbles hot under her soles. Under her left arm, she carried the giant mouse. With her free hand she led the bicorn after her. Her chest was bursting as she rounded the corner to Bartholomus's house, and saw the royal carriage drawn up outside. Gasping, she ran to the gate.

Princess Carina stood on the narrow patch of lawn, flanked by two soldiers, her cheeks as pink as her silk dress. Her fingers were bejewelled with rings, her neck encircled with a thick gold necklace.

At her feet, Bartholomus knelt in the dirt of a flowerbed. Beside him lay a garden trowel and some abandoned seedlings. Such commonplace items,

and yet as she saw them Henna's eyes blurred.

Bartholomus bowed his head. "Your Highness, if you would only——"

"Silence!" Carina slapped him across the face. "I'm not interested in your excuses. Guards!"

"Your Highness?" Henna pushed the gate open. "I have a gift for you."

Carina's gaze flicked contemptuously over Henna's bedraggled tunic and the ungainly mouse clasped under her arm, then settled on the fantastical creature beside her. She licked her lips like a cat spying prey, and stepped over to the gate. "A pretty enough toy, but I'm not interested in two-horned miniature freaks. I require a full grown unicorn."

"Really?" Henna feigned surprise. "I could make one for Your Highness, but we would need privacy. It is impossible to create a true unicorn in the presence of men."

Henna held her breath. She saw Carina glance over the cowering magus and then back at the gleaming bicorn.

"You could make this unicorn now?" asked Carina.

"Within five minutes, if we are alone."

"Guards, take the old man and——"

Henna cleared her throat noisily.

"Was there something else, witch?"

"Naturally, I have no intention of troubling Your Highness for payment. Yet I did hope that you might release the magus as a gesture of . . . good will."

Carina's eyes narrowed, but she turned to the guards. "Let the old man go, and wait for me in the carriage. Now, witch, get on with it."

Already tracing a pentacle on the

lawn, Henna murmured, "I need to borrow a token of yours, so that I may bind the unicorn to you. Something you value, perhaps a necklace."

Carina undid the clasp of her gold necklace, and tossed it onto the grass.

"Come a little closer, Your Highness. That's better." Carefully, Henna positioned the giant mouse within the star. "Mus, Mus, Carina—"

Sunlight sparkled on the necklace, burst into dazzling gold fire. Henna shut her eyes, the afterimage of the flames dancing across her vision. When she looked back, the necklace was gone.

Princess Carina's nose wrinkled strangely. She hopped forward and gave a loud and most undignified squeek.

Henna grinned. "Princess Carina?"

The princess only squeeked, but Henna wasn't looking at the other woman. Her eyes were intent on the mouse. As she watched, it struggled to stand on its hind legs, its whiskered face contorting with rage, and then nipped her sharply on the ankle.

"Ouch! Behave yourself, otherwise you won't get any supper." Henna scooped the mouse up, and went over to the carriage.

"Guards! A terrible thing has happened. The unicorn spurned the princess. Naturally, she demanded an explanation." Lowering her head, Henna whispered, "And I had to tell her that rejections only occur if the lady is unchaste. I'm afraid the shock has unhinged Her Highness's senses."

THAT YEAR'S Midsummer Festival was the gayest in living memory. Henna strolled through the brightly colored pavilions, sipping the magus's fine elderberry wine, and watching the merriment. For the ladies of the court danced and cavorted, giggled and flirted with a new and infectious lightness of heart.

The king suspected what had happened, but he made no mention of it. It's a delicate matter trying to prove that your daughter is a virgin, particularly if the entire court has seen her flirting with minstrels. Besides which, his daughter was much less trouble than ever before. For all the Princess Carina desired were the rich and varied cheeses heaped high on the banquet tables. ∎

© DONALD W. SCHANK

Biological Imperative
by John Everson

Something was burning, what I couldn't tell. The stench came fast, strong—rubber mixed with electricity, I thought. But before I could so much as radio a distress or look around the cabin to see what was flaming itself, the flyer took a heavy nosedive and a blink later my nostrils were spurting blood on the boards."

"And this was over the ExKar Swamp area?" Marvis interrupted.

Marvis was a corpulent, pompous fool. He was also Hope settlement commander by some twisted quirk of irony. Anyone on base—including me—would have been better suited to run the place than him. But he had the colored blocks on his lapel and I didn't. Rank stank. I conceded that yes, my flyer had decided to commit suicide over the ExKar Swamp.

"I pumped the throttle, hit the flap adjusts, even flipped on autopilot, but every switch on the dash was dead. I was just about in kissing distance with puke yellow bubbles in the froth of the swamp and knew there was only one way out of this one. Manual eject."

"But you still did not radio a distress?" Marvis interrupted again. I smiled at what I figured must be a lump of rock hiding behind his glossy bare forehead.

"No sir. I had maybe ten seconds to blow clear after I realized the entire electronics system had choked, and I assumed the radio, which, as you know is driven by the same system, was also dead. And even if it wasn't, by the time I'd have made the call, I would have been ten feet underground. I pulled the space-me cord and was thrown clear as the flyer plowed into the swamp."

"If you were ejected safely, how did you break your leg?"

This guy was a complete empty! I decided that there was no lump of rock under that sweaty dome. Just air. Ejected safely, my ass. Who ever heard of a "safe" eject at 140 mph?

Konners came, with false benevolence, to my rescue.

"Sir," the young lieutenant asked quietly. He had hopes of a power climb, and did not want to rub Marvy-Marvis the wrong way. Saying anything took a form of guts, I suppose.

"Why don't we have Cale tell the story start to finish, and cross examine when he's through," Konners proposed. "I think it will speed things up."

Thanks, Konners, I thought. Butt-sniffing jackal. I knew Konners was only shutting up the rockhead so they could get to the part where they said, "Cale Loggins, you are hereby sentenced to death by disrupter fire . . ." I nodded my gratitude at Konners and continued.

"My head smashed into the cockpit cover as my seat was launched from the flyer, and for a moment, everything went black and white. At once, I completely understood what people mean when they say they saw stars. I saw supernovae. And then, before my vision could clear, before I could pull my 'chute cord, my body smashed into something and I heard a crack. It seemed to come from far away, that snap, but in my head I knew it was me that had just been broken. I was dazed, didn't know what had snapped, couldn't move to see. And before the pain even reached my brain, I went zombie.

I DON'T know how long I was out, but the next thing I remember it was night. I opened my eyes and for a minute, I was sure I'd been blinded. There was nothing. No stars, no clouds, no silhouettes of trees nearby. Nothing. I tried raising my arm to see if I could see my hand, but it didn't move. The other one did, and better still, I could see it, just barely. Then, deep-stare on the utterly black horizon, I could make out a dot or two of light. It was early night, I realized, since we were facing into the Oris cloud. By two or three in the morning those stars would be shining down on me.

But I wanted to know how bad things were before then. Slivers of agony were punching their way up and down my nerves from all parts of my body except my right arm, which I couldn't feel at all. My heart did double time as I realized it must have been sheared off in the eject, and I was probably bleeding out my last ounces of life right now. I wouldn't make it to see the stars overhead again.

Gingerly, I probed with my good hand across my chest and found my right armpit, which still seemed attached to something. I followed it up the cold flesh of my bicep and located my elbow pointing to Sirius behind my head. I was laying on it and had put it to sleep, I realized, and laughed out loud. Just once. The resulting pain in my chest told me there was a rib or two no longer happy whole, and the shooting pains that signaled the return of sensation to my right arm as I pulled it out from behind my head and let it flop uselessly to the ground were none too laughable either.

So, I thought, two usable arms and some bad ribs. I ought to be able to travel if I went slow, taking care not to puncture a lung in the process. I laid there until the tingles subsided, and carefully began to push myself upright. The pain in my chest may have been enough to stop me anyway, but it was then that I realized some of that knifing pain was coming from my left leg. I did another hand probe and felt something sharp just below by knee. It wasn't a wayward stick. My hand came back warm and sticky and somehow that just seemed a cue for the pain. It stabbed. I blacked.

IT WAS in the deep red of morning when I woke again. My body throbbed and my tongue felt thick with thirst.

Everything was silent. For the first time, I realized that I'd miraculously been thrown clear of the swamp. Its yellow scum bubbled to my right, mere feet away. I lay helpless in a clearing between the deadly swamp and the questionable safety of jumble vines that rose like orchid mountains yards to my left. I could smell their dangerously pungent fruit carried through the air in waves, a cloying mix of bad eggs and perfume, and my stomach rumbled. It was hard to believe I'd survived the night exposed as I was, but I wasn't naive enough to believe that luck would hold. With lurches and some involuntary screams, I began to drag myself towards the vines.

I worked as an upside down crab, my elbows and ass absorbing most of the bumps, but I could feel my ribs grinding and see the sharp white sliver of bone shifting in and out of my coveralls. I passed out again twice before collapsing just inside the shelter of the purple vine hills. I didn't know if the crabcrawlers could forage this far from the swamp, but fervently hoped they couldn't. Because I wasn't moving another foot.

I also didn't want to get too far from the clearing. If there was a rescue team out, they'd never find me. So with my head propped against the fuzzy purple root stem of a jumble vine and my feet sticking out under the crimson sun, I crashed out again.

The heavy stillness of the night woke me again. Out there, beyond the dome—the darkness is so thick, it's . . . heart-stopping. I know, you've seen it here from the base—but there's always a light somewhere, if not full hallway illumination or a bedroom desklamp,

you have the LED of a clock or the green and red blips on your room intercom. Out there, under the empty sky, no stars, no nightlights, no defense, I shivered in utter terror. I knew that sooner or later, if I survived long enough to see it, the vampire skitters would come swarming out of the sky to peck my body to bones as they do to the Konarbi. And they wouldn't care whether I stayed alive to watch my disembowelment. It was then, at the moment I decided that I would never be found, that I would be eaten as surely as a Konarbi caught on the open plain, that I heard the voice.

Food for Esku, I will not have you be.

There was no sound, the air was a blank slate. *The voice was in my head.* I was not even going to last long enough to go as graceful carrion. I was headed for complete loon-dom before morning.

Though, you must have water, or you will soon be food for swampsnakes.

No shit, I thought at my new head friend. And where will I be getting a nice refreshing bucket of H$_2$O? Maybe a little face dunk into the yellow swamp? And maybe afterwards pull back my skull without a face?

Open your mouth.

I don't know why I did. Delirium, maybe. I was curious to see how my schizoid invisible pal would make water appear out of the air. But as I split my fevered lips apart, there was a rustling in the vines next to me, and before I could so much as scream—which is exactly what my throat was gearing up to do—my throat was drowning in a splash of cool, wonderful water. It ran out of my outh and into my ears, trickled into my nose and made me sneeze. It dampened my fevered forehead. It was heavenly. I forgot my fear and thirstily gulped the liquid as it continued to rain down over my face. I could feel it travel the length of my esophagus, cooling and soothing until at last it hit my deflated stomach, sloshing around like beer in a keg. It stopped then, and as I licked the last drops from my chapped lips, I saw for the first time my savior. Or at least, its silhouette.

It massed the material of three or four good-sized men and in the darkness seemed only a giant amorphous blob. Black on black. And it spoke again into my head.

You are from the shining circle . . . strange lights?

I saw the picture of the Hope settlement dome in my mind and nodded, unseen in the night. "Yes," I croaked. "Are you a Konarbi?"

There was puzzled silence, as in my mind I tried to remember, as best I could, one of the Konarbi we filmed being eaten to death by the needle-beaked vampire skitters.

I felt a sadness not my own at the image, and realized that this Konarbi could catch some of my thoughts as well as speak in them. Then the being affirmed my hypothesis. *Yes. Esku eat . . . Konarbi.*

My stomach lurched then, and as the pain shot through my leg I vomited the too-quickly swallowed contents of my stomach onto the ground. The Konarbi backed into the brush at my sickness, but I—how can I say this? Like a filter over my eyes, I could feel its presence nearby. I slipped into the black again, but my fear had vanished.

WHEN I came to again it was full daylight, and in spite of the heat, I was shaking. Every shiver grated my leg bones together and several times, I cried out so loud echoes came back to me from across the swamp. I knew I was going to die. It had been at least two days, and nobody had found me. I was afraid to move into the cool shelter of the jumble vines for fear of predation. Yet I was vulnerable to the vampire skitters—Esku—in the open. I considered simply rolling into the swamp and ending it fast, but, call it cowardice or self-preservation instinct, I couldn't go through with it. So I lay there, baking and shivering in the sun, alone but for the kindly night ministrations of a globular Konarbi. Or had I dreamed that whole episode?

That's what I'd convinced myself of by the time nightfall returned again. I was crying as the purple glow yielded to black and still no help arrived. And then I felt a pressure on my vision—a tapping of my mind, I guess you'd say. And the jumble vines rustled once more. The Konarbi had returned.

You must kill me and eat my flesh, the creature announced.

Not 'Hi, how was your day?' It offered itself as rations from word one. I laughed. It continued.

If you are to survive until rescue, you must have sustenance. I must soon die anyway and you may provide a clean death. Therefore, why not serve both of our needs?

In my head I felt the rightness of this solution, the beauty of a perfect answer. On some level, I knew that this was not my own feeling, but I also knew somehow with some deep sensitivity that this was what the creature not wanted—needed.

"It is against my law to kill another thinking being," I began to explain, and a rumble filled my brain.

You will learn another law if your kind is to stay here, the thunder spoke behind my eyes. *If this solution is right, you will have a place. If not?*

I suddenly saw our dome crushed, as if by an invisible hand. Esku swarmed from the sky, and fleeing men were pecked down by the unstoppable arrows of their mouths. In seconds, I saw human carrion lying in a ragged line about the dome, a dozen Esku to each corpse. And in the distance, in a chilling silent circle, a ring of bloblike Konarbi watched motionless.

Tears were rolling unheeded from my eyes as I begged for explanation. "Why would you do this? We have tried to leave you to your lives and only observe. We do not interfere."

Interfere now, the voice in my head tolled. *Or die. You make this choice here. They will make this choice there. Use your weapon now and end my life. Eat of my flesh to keep you alive until your rescue. More than I watch here.*

With a shaking hand, I pulled my pulse pistol from its holster and aimed it at the ill-defined blob to my right. In the steadily darkening night I could barely make out its differing blackness from that of the heavy sky.

"If I kill you, won't other Konarbi come to kill me?" I asked.

No. Use your weapon. Preserve yourself. Know that you are doing me a . . . kindness. Be quick. Be alive.

I felt the pressure on me intensifying, not forcing me to press the button, but nudging me, begging me, pleading . . .

I did.

The light needled from the gun into the side of the nebulous creature and it seemed to, deflate, somewhat. In my head I felt, for an instant, its pain. And then as the pressure lifted, a last gasp of happiness? Relief? Thanks?

I DON'T know. Somehow, killing the Konarbi made me feel right. And it took a few hours, but I did, eventually, carve off some chunks of its hide. To this day I don't know if it was blind hunger or a compulsion the Konarbi put on me, but I sliced it up like a side of beef. The meat was bloodless, with a taste like, I don't know—mustard and bitter spices. I only ate a couple bites the first time. Then I lay awake agonizing for hours about whether those bites would kill me in a worse way than the pain I was already dying from. When day came and I was still alive—now with a belly aching for more food. I carved off some more of the dead Konarbi and ate again."

"And just how many times did you go back to the Konarbi cafeteria before Corporal Jackcin located you?" Marvis interrupted.

"I don't know," I shrugged. "Several. Things were pretty blurry by the time Jackcin showed up."

Things were pretty blurry for quite a while afterwards too, as they ripped open my leg to set it correctly in sickbay, and then nursed me back to health for weeks, just so I'd be ready to stand court martial and be put to death. For the hundredth time I tried to fathom the Konarbi's motives for forcing me into murder, for choosing suicide at the hands of an alien.

Was it selflessness? Did the Konarbi truly believe that, human codes or not, its death was the only way I could survive? And if so, why was my life so important? And in spite of the Konarbi's actions, here I was facing death for the murder of a sentient alien; an alien that had begged me to take its life.

Marvis grinned at me, his crooked teeth so full of fake pity that I had to feel sorry for myself. Somebody had to. I was for sure going to die for saving myself. I should have just rolled into the swamp. But as I despaired, the alien's phrase came unbidden to my mind.

More than I watch here. What did it mean?

"If you expect us to believe that an alien crawled up alongside you and told you to eat it, you're too crazy to live anyway," Marvis drawled, winding up for the kill. "And if you can't pilot a flyer without crashing it, well, you don't belong here. I'm invoking article 9, paragraph 2 of the settlement law. Any human that viciously takes the life of a known sentient creature is subject to the same penalties as those for the murder of a human. In this dome, that means death."

Marvis grinned, his cheeks lifting subtley from their usual ravines of sloth. "Konners, take him to lock-up. Execution for dawn."

I didn't struggle as ass-kiss Konners shoved me down the corridor. There was no escape here. In a dome with two hundred people on a planet of airborne killers where I knew neither the flora nor the fauna that would allow me the sustenance for a dubious survival, escape was simply not in the equation. Marvis had despised me from the minute my commission brought me here, and I must admit, the feeling had been mutually stoked.

"You gonna smile as they shoot me up, or will it be you tamping the needle?" I asked Konners sweetly. But before he could answer I added. "Oh, I'm sorry, you'll be so busy tonguing Marvis clean you won't be able to enjoy the little death orgy, will you?"

I got a punch in the kidneys for my effort. Not a reward I would recommend chasing.

My cell was much like any cell in history. Four blank walls, a dirty floor and a ceiling. Mine had a luminous square for light up top and a bunk suspended from one wall. A waste disposal shoot decorated a corner. Nope. Some aspects of civilization do not change. Only this cell was not designed to accommodate the mole "tunneling to freedom a spoon at a time" prisoner. No cracks, no tile, no escape. And again, where would I go if I could?

I laid back on the bunk and considered again the few words I had traded with the Konarbi. Why did it give its life for mine? What did it have to gain? What had I gained by the exchange? The chance to die in another fashion, apparently.

THAT NIGHT I dreamed of Konarbi. Hundreds of them, rolling and plowing through the jumble vines to emerge on a great open plain. The sky glowed with the eerie iridescence of the Konar sun and then, suddenly, the glow was dimmed. The sky flooded with dark shapes, and a flock of needles dove into the helpless Konarbi caravan. In minutes the plain was filled with pulsing, dying, shreds of flesh. I woke from the dream in tears of shared pain.

And heard the dome attack alarm system clanging.

For the second time in a day I heard an echo in my brain. Something the Konarbi had said to me before I'd killed it.

More than I watch here.

It was them causing the alarm, I knew it was. They had come for me. They had seen my murderous act, read it in my mind, and they had come for their own vengeance.

Before I had time to call for a guard to get the scoop, Konners appeared at my cell. A guard keyed open the lock and opened the door.

The little shit looked happy! The base was apparently under attack, and he was smiling his beady eyes out. But he didn't say a word.

Instead he pushed me through back corridors until we arrived at the command station. Marvis was waiting there, his back to us. I quickly saw the object of his concentration. Or should I say, objects. The Konarbi had come. There on the gray-green plain, a vast crowd gathered, ten, maybe fifteen Konarbi deep.

Marvis turned to me, the fat of his face a ruddy mix of anger and confusion. "You killed one of them," he coughed at me. A finger trembled at his side before rising to cut the air between us. "You brought them here, and now you can send them away."

"Or die trying," murmured Konners.

Marvis tossed me a link. "Get out there; find out what they want, and get them to back off. I'll be listening. Don't

come back until they're gone."

"Does this mean you're suspending my sentence?" I challenged him.

"Kick him out the lock," Marvis growled to Konners.

In minutes I was standing on the wrong side of the dome, staring down a wall of silently heaving flesh.

I didn't know what to say. Communicating with irregular lumps of breathing alien were not my training specialty. For lack of a better opening, I said "Hi."

At me word, a dozen of the smaller lumps glided forward on their ciliated feet. They crossed the twenty yards between the Konarbi and me with amazing speed, stopping in a semicircle at my feet. In my mind, I suddenly saw a picture of the alien I had killed, but it seemed different somehow, more sunken than when I'd left it . . .

The testing was successful, a voice suddenly announced in my brain. This talking without words took a little getting used to, I thought, shaking my head in consternation.

At your feet is the result of your action.

I stared at the pulsing globes around my boots in dawning comprehension.

I spoke with the being—I don't know which one of the Konarbi mob the voice came from, maybe all of them—for a long time. The link beeped urgently in my pocket, but I ignored Marvis. Let him steam. From his view, I stood out there simply staring at the creatures for fifteen or twenty minutes.

At the end of our talk (think?) I nodded to the assemblage and turned away. There was a moment of shared sadness and hope so commingled, I could never hope to explain it. We stood on the brink of either foolhardy disaster or a strange new companionship.

"EVERY PERSON in the dome must take a pistol outside, approach a Konarbi, and kill it," I announced to Marvis when I returned. I don't think I'd ever seen him laugh in such pure derision before that moment. It did not improve his looks. When his jowls settled, I tried to explain.

"The Konarbi who came to me was an experiment. They didn't know if there was some necessity to their being murdered by the Esku for reproduction. Apparently, there is not, since I just met the children which resulted from my killing of the Konarbi by the swamp."

Marvis was looking at me like I was daft. He was not tracking the direction here.

"Listen," I urged him. "The Konarbi are intelligent. But they lack the means to kill themselves. In order to reproduce, they *must be killed.* If they wait to die from old age, nothing happens. The *violence* triggers something in their bodies which causes eggs to form in the dying body, and those eggs feed on its bulk until ready to hatch. But even if they wanted to refuse to reproduce, and simply hid from their one enemy, the Esku, the Konarbi could not. When their bodies reach a certain level of maturity, they instinctually begin yearning for the open plains—where the Esku wait. When a Konarbi gives in to that instinctual call, it is dead —and young will rise from its carcass days after it has been slaughtered."

I could see Marvis was starting to wonder if I could possibly be telling the truth. But the shift in his eyes said he still thought I was pulling something.

"Where do we come into all this?" he asked.

"We can provide a cleaner, less painful death than the Esku. Also, we won't kill the children, as the Esku often wait around to do. We would be both reaper and birther."

"And if we don't agree to be Konarbi executioners?" Konners chimed.

"They will destroy the dome and with their numbers gathered, lure the Esku here to kill us all," I replied.

As if to underscore my statement, a dull boom echoed through the walls. First Watch Leffer's voice clicked in over the 'com:

"Commander Marvis. The Konarbi have begun ramming the southeast wall. The walls won't stand up to this concerted attack long, sir. They're already denting." Another boom moved through the air.

"And why can't *you* simply go out there and cut 'em up for us?" Marvis barked, turning to me.

"They demand that, as a show of partnership, we all take some of the responsibility. If we don't want this to become a war instead of an alliance, we'll do it as they ask, sir. They speak to each other as they've spoken to me. That means with a loose mental network, every Konarbi on this planet knows what is happening here now. They have not approached this lightly, and I recommend that we do not either."

Marvis stared unmoving out at the aliens.

"Sir," I said softly. "Why don't you go speak with them yourself?"

After a moment, he stabbed at the 'com and rounded up his favorite team of bullies (some called them advisors, but I say, spade's a spade . . .) and five minutes later the group was stalking out the lock to chat with the Konarbi. Five minutes after that, and Marvis was calling for every available hand to evacuate the dome, armed for action.

"Every hand but Cale," he amended with some irritation.

Thank you, I breathed, wondering why the Konarbi had spared me. I knew it had to have been them who insisted on it. Marvis would have liked to have had me kill them all myself!

You have done enough for now, answered a familiar voice deep in my head.

I don't know how Marvis explained things to the rest of the base. Maybe he didn't—maybe each Konarbi chose its own executioner and gave its own explanations. But an hour later, the plain outside our base was covered with dead Konarbi and dazed earthmen.

I got it all on vid. You never know when you might need some evidence to hold over your commanding officer, especially when he's never officially removed a death penalty from your head. And incoming Earth ships would *not* understand!

Despite their explanations, I couldn't help but feel a raw twinge of sadness as I watched the slaughter. I tried to convince myself that it was kinder this way. They didn't suffer as they did from the Esku. We were entering, in a way, this planet's biosphere, at last. The children of these Konarbi would feel a strange kinship to us, and most likely return to us when it was their time to die—and spawn. But I swallowed a lump as I saw Marvis' pistol burn the life from one of the aliens. What if the people in the dome grew to enjoy this?

It's a biological imperative, the voice had explained in my head.

But that didn't mean I had to feel good about it. ■

Unnatural Balances
by Jim Lee

Gasping, Matthew Bezek awoke. The disturbing images slowly faded from his consciousness. He made no effort to hold onto them. His new reality was quite bad enough.

Kimberly was still at his side, though now upright and frowning. The tips of her widespread fingers rested lightly on his chest. She touched him gingerly, still untrusting of her retractable claws. Matthew found the gentle uncertainty of that touch painful as an unspoken accusation.

He swept her hand aside, turned to the bare wall. His enhanced vision penetrated the murk, revealing every detail of the grimy cinderblocks before him.

Better to face that, instead of her misplaced compassion.

A low-frequency growl, too faint for human ears to discern, made him turn back. Matthew and Kimberly exchanged quick, questioning glances. He nodded and she answered the throaty rumble in kind, her palate moist with anticipation.

The trap door opened silently and their meal was lowered into their arms. Donetta waited fifteen seconds for them to clear the way. Then she joined them, landing smartly on the sub-basement's floor. She paused an instant, grinning at her "kids" and their barely controlled hunger.

Effortlessly, Donetta moved the heavy crates into position, scaled them and raised a meaty hand. She secured the secret entranceway after sniffing the air, round eyes shifting back and forth. Satisfied, she climbed down and knelt beside the kill.

Donetta took a slow breath and extended her talons.

It was the signal Kimberly and Matthew waited for. Both dove forward, ripping pale hunks of meat loose and feeding with naked desperation.

Donetta sat on her haunches, studying her young ones as she dined. The one proven and confident hunter here, she could afford a measure of decorum. But providing all the fresh meat for three was becoming tiresome.

And traces of inappropriate squeamishness persisted—despite the apparent feeding frenzy, Matthew and Kimberly still avoided the head, the face.

Wielding her claws with surgical skill, Donetta carved out the pancreas, a favored organ, and consumed it in slow, even bites. Her grunt commanded immediate attention.

"Ready," she announced, smacking her wide lips. "Both of you."

Blood on their lips and trailing unevenly down their chins, Donetta's "kids" looked even paler than usual.

"It's only been two weeks," Matthew pointed out.

"We heal quick," Donetta responded. She swatted him across his recently broken arm to prove the point.

He winced, though not from physical discomfort.

"Tomorrow night," Donetta concluded, gazing steadily into their eyes. "Me and you and you. And the Hunt."

Donetta shifted, cut a fleshy wad from her kill's thigh and flicked it into her mouth, discussion over.

TWENTY HOURS later, Matthew Bezek sniffed the air and grimaced. The scent of a passing truck's diesel engine disgusted him as never before. He inched deeper into the shadows and brushed against Kimberly.

They crouched together for a time in companionable silence.

There was no telling how long Donetta would be. The slow, barely audible rhythm of Kimberly's breathing and the reassuring warmth of her body lulled him.

Without being conscious of it, Matthew stared through the darkness. He saw past the trash-strewn alley and beyond, far beyond the confines of that decaying inner city. A waking dream came over him, more vivid than any of his mightmares.

It was fifteen years and several hundred miles ago. In the mountains. He and his Dad, alone across an open campfire. Their first hunting trip.

Sounds accompanied the image. The crackle, pop and hiss of the fire. The whispering murmur of a voice. A strong and familiar voice.

Something squirmed from a crevice of Matthew's brain, assumed an instant and ironic reality. He gave his head a shake, wet his lips. He closed his eyes, but that only intensified the experience.

"Nature." Matt, Senior spoke clearly. He studied his son across the dancing flames and across the years. "It has its own subtle, gorgeous balance."

The man across the way from Matthew was stout and vigorous. Unaware of what was to come. Deep brown eyes sparkled, reflected the golden shimmer of the campfire. Or was it simply that his eyes had always gleamed and glittered like that, as he held forth on his favorite topic?

"Nature's balance," the ghost image said again, rubbing a wide hip that, for the moment, seemed all-too-substantial. "Most pay it lip-service at best, son. But to be a truly responsible and worthy part of the living world, you gotta understand and appreciate it. And, most of all, do what you can to protect it!"

"Protect it," Matthew whispered to himself. He tasted something bitter—and inescapable. "Not run from it."

"Matthew?" The pads of her fingers probed him and it was a relief to be drawn back. Not much of one, though.

Their shared fate was his fault. His choice, even.

Feelings of guilt and of responsibility, rational and otherwise, piled up behind his eyes. They became a bleak internal mountain, a jagged peak. A certain deathtrap for his soul.

Then she nudged him again. Lightly. The way she always did whenever he sank into despair, drowning in his loss. The deep, dark pool of his loss.

Metaphors, Matthew thought. The Old Man was always big on metaphors. And now he's passed another of his fixations along to me. Like a communicable disease.

Matthew's eyes snapped open. Even as he tilted his head to offer his thanks, their enhanced hearing warned of another's approach. It couldn't be Donetta. There was no grace, no cunning to the stumbling footfalls.

'Should we hide?' Kimberly mouthed the question, eyes bright with fear. Neither of them had faced a normal human being since the Change.

Matthew shook his head. He took her hand and squeezed it, careful of her healing wounds. There was nothing obvious about them to arouse suspicion. Not even the color of their skin. It was, after all, a multi-racial neighborhood.

The unshaved, foul-smelling man staggering down the alley carried with him the air of death forthcoming. It excited them, instinctively. Matthew and Kimberly trembled, held each other in a close crouch and struggled to keep their talons sheathed.

The stranger saw them lurking in the shadows and passed without a word. He clutched the quarter-full bottle of Thunderbird with mindless jealousy. Rheumy eyes and nose, an uncertain gait all were testimony to the fortified wine's power.

Matthew and Kimberly stared after him. They were still capable of loathing their new drives. And of feeling a kind of empathy for a being once like themselves.

They moved closer, as if the night chill might still trouble them. Kimberly's blue-jeaned buttocks pressed gingerly against Matthew's thigh, seeking only his comfort and understanding. He responded, slowly folded his slightly stiff arm across her equally tender midsection.

All but the worst injuries were little more than memories by now. Like the accident itself. As Donetta observed, they were quick to heal.

Unnaturally so, Matthew thought sardonically.

"Can we do it?" Kimberly whispered. She adjusted the set of his fingers away from the still-sore spot where a splintered rib had shredded the side of one lung. The air-sack and the ribcage were both restored, the broken pieces of bone dissolved and re-absorbed by her altered body. "Can we, Matt? Really?"

"We've been doing it." The reply was soft and grim. "For two weeks now, sweetness." The last word stuck in his throat and Matthew had to force it out.

He could recall the flavor of her mouth with maddening clarity. But could he ever put his lips to hers again?

"No." She shifted, her long hair rustling against his chin. "Not that. I mean... Matt, the actual... I don't think... I don't know if I *can*!" Her words dried up, even as she began to sob.

Matthew nodded, kissed the back of her head. That part of her still seemed clean. The straight black silk of her hair was devoid of the pervasive death-house odor. At least so far.

"Don't think of it as killing, Kim. Like Donetta says, we're as much scavengers as predators."

"Bull!" she protested, pushing his arm away so abruptly he winced. Never aging, they could still know pain. Of all kinds. Salt water ran down what was once a young woman's face. "They're walking around, Matt. Thinking, feeling creatures..."

"But not alive," Matthew hissed, his tone sharpened to a fine edge. She was voicing his deepest and most troubling thoughts, so he had to lash back. He had to crush them, before they gained the upperhand and left him powerless. "Damn it, Kim! Undead. By definition, not alive! Dangerous. Dead and deadly. And ... not human."

"Neither are we, now."

Matthew turned away.

He put his head against a dirty wall. He

closed his eyes and another memory, more unwelcome than any other, demanded his attention. It hissed and spat at him, until he let it come.

His Dad, again. But a more recent image. Last year, in the hospital. The robust body, wasted and destroyed. A victim of the tiny sneak-thief——a retrovirus, a thing only semi-living and utterly thoughtless.

Matthew faced Kimberly, his cheeks as damp as hers.

Bad enough, watching his father go like that. And then, just as he put it behind him, there was that rain-slick roadway and his own late-night impatience. A sharp curve. A jutting fragment of an old wall. The ruptured tank, spewing gasoline.

And only Donetta to pull them free.

"I had no right," he murmured. "To decide for you."

"I was unconscious," Kimberly conceded. "You wanted to live, wanted me to live. I know that, Matt. I understand. And Donetta…"

"Should've let us both die, Kim. Like we were meant to. That's what you really think, isn't it?"

Her oval face was serious, though not lacking compassion. "It's done. I accept it, Matt. Really. And I can see her side, too. How lonely it must've been for her ——alone all those years!"

Matthew nodded.

Donetta went way back. She claimed to be perhaps the last survivor of the time when raids on human cemetaries provided the fresh cadavers they required. It took both time and conscious effort to adapt, to save themselves from humanity's organized fury and to carve out a small but important new niche in the supernatural food chain.

Over the centuries, humanity forgot them. Still more recently, the hemovores themselves had been dismissed from human awareness. The stubborn power of the Aging Ones' disbelief was amazing, even to Donetta.

She muttered about it more than once in the presence of her new "kids."

But Matthew suddenly had his own ideas about that and he couldn't wait for Donetta's return to share them. He took Kimberly by the shoulder, looked deep into her almond eyes. His voice rose higher than he wished and vibrated with intensity.

"It's worth it, Kim. No matter how ugly, how unsavory it seems. We're the human race's silent partners, now. Their only allies in a war so ancient and weird, they can't even remember or accept it as real! That's what you've got to cling to, Kim. If it wasn't for us, those damned vamp——"

"Idiot!"

The single word cut through the night, slashing. Like a dagger. It gouged the air right out of Matthew's lungs and silenced him. He and Kimberly scrambled to their feet, wheeled to face their mentor.

Donetta emerged from the gloom, squinting and curling her wide lip in annoyance. She was stocky and her skin was half a shade darker than the drunk who'd passed minutes before. She looked to be in her early fifties, which meant very little.

"Idiot white boy! Keep your mouth shut when out in the open!"

Matthew pursed his lips. "Sorry. But we would've heard if anybody came…"

"Like you heard me?" Donetta stepped closer, let him see her upraised hand, the faint glint of partially extended claws.

Matthew winced. "Okay. It was my fault."

"Maybe. But if not, you'd still take the blame." A bit of the immediate menace left her. Donetta turned toward Kimberly. "He always do that, China Doll? Protect you, take all the heat himself?"

Kimberly shrugged and Donetta's head snapped back around.

"Bring the supplies. And keep your mouth shut."

"You found one?" Kimberly gasped.

Donetta's eyes glowed. "Not jus' one, baby-girl. Whole pack's out tonight. Hungry as they get, too. 'Nough to make a mistake or two, I hope. Come on." She gestured and was off, gliding silently through the darkness.

Matthew hefted the duffel bag and followed Donetta's confident stride. Kimberly brought up the rear, fingering the small cross that dangled from her throat.

They proceeded three blocks east and four south, took cover in the remains of a burned-out building. They peered across the way, into an unlit city parklet.

Matthew counted—nine, ten, eleven vampires. Six female and five male, all full-sized adults. They swarmed and fought over a pair of limp, slightly smaller bodies. The way they snarled and jostled for position reminded Matthew of the spotted hyenas in the TV documentary Matt, Senior had made Matthew watch with him two nights before his Dad's death. It was almost the last thing, the last sight the two of them had shared.

Matthew tensed, his talons came out and he lunged for a weapon. A crucifix, a stake carved with Druid power symbols —anything! He hissed when Donetta caught his arm and shook her head.

"They're just kids," he whispered bitterly.

Donetta answered, even softer and with no emotion. "More adolescents, I'd say. And see those scraps, what they were dressed in? Colors, Matthew. Couple junior gang-bangers. Nobody'll miss 'em much."

Matthew's stare broadcast his thoughts.

"Dead already, Matt. Drained. Besides, it's not our place, protecting humans from their own stupidity."

"Not our place?" His whisper barely choked back Matthew's rage. "What is our 'place,' then? Why save us at all? Why Change us?"

"Company, like Kim said." Donetta's eyes returned to study the distant carnage. "And the local food supply more than allowed for it. Well, look at 'em. Think they *like* having to work together, share their kills? No way. They're pure hunters, loners. Unlike us, Matthew."

Matthew stared across the way and thought about the fresh-killed hemovores Donetta had brought them. All gaunt, painfully thin—same as the ones he saw now. He chewed his lip. Then he murmured, "Too many predators for the population base? How many vampires in this city?"

Donetta shrugged. "Couple hundred, easy."

Kimberly inched close enough to join the muffled conversation. "There's thousands of people here. How can a few hundred be too many?"

"Just are, baby-girl. Just are."

"She's right, Kim. There can never be more than a tiny fraction of hunters to the hunted. Not if things are going to be in anything like the . . . proper balance." He stopped, only now grasping the implications. He eyed Donetta closely. "The population got out of control, with only you to cull them back. You needed help."

"Only thing to do," she admitted.

They locked eyes for a long, silent moment.

It was Kimberly who thought to look

back, across her shoulder. She sucked in her breath. "They're splitting up."

Matthew's face twisted. "Carrying off the bodies?"

"Sure." Donetta whispered in his ear. "Can't leave evidence. Bunch of corpses drained of blood start turning up, the Aging Ones might just *have* to face the truth. If they do, it's back to vampire hunting. And these days, the humans have the means to finish 'em for good."

"Would that be so bad, Donetta?"

She looked at him, sniffed, "I'd rather not starve, white boy."

They watched, then followed a pair of females who carried the larger of the night's victims down a narrow alley. The bloodless burden slowed the hemovores and mostly full bellies left them less alert than usual. Donetta used hand signals to arrange the ambush and divide the contents of Matthew's duffel bag.

The young ghouls followed their prey at a safe distance as Donetta circled for a frontal assault.

Matthew watched Donetta fling herself into action from a fire escape, landing directly in front of the lead vampire. A splash of holy water blinded the undead blonde and a savage blow tore one side of her face. The blonde dropped the dead human's feet and snarled, her fangs flashing in the moonlight.

Now Matthew and Kimberly made their move, rushing the other vampire from behind. They had a huge advantage, what with their target tossing aside her burden and darting forward, focused entirely on Donetta and the blonde. But the sudden excitement of their first Hunt was too much——Kimberly and Matthew both snarled loud battlecries.

Warned, the dark-haired vampire whirled. She jumped sideways, bowled over Kimberly. Her fangs sank deep into Kimberly's arm and a jerk of the head tore flesh. Frantic and unthinking, Matthew tried to pry the brunette off barehanded, instead of using the weapons crammed under his belt. His razored talons opened deep slash wounds on the hemovore's back and arms, but did no critical damage.

The brunette elbowed him in the gut, rolled free as Kimberly grabbed for the stake and mallet she'd lost control of. The toe of the vampire's boot caught Matthew's groin and he doubled over.

Kimberly saw their prey draw herself up and instinct said the vampire was about to transform for escape. "No damn way!" Kimberly screamed and she dove on the brunette, used the stake more as a club than a spear.

The vampire threw her aside and met Matthew's next charge, delivering a blow that cracked two of the young ghoul's incredibly strong ribs. Her fangs raked his cheek, punctured a small vein in his neck. A blind, flailing hand tore part of his right earlobe off.

Then Matthew was tossed aside. He looked up, saw Donetta drive a specially blessed wooden dagger of Hindu origin into the vampire's side. She was able to pinion the thrashing brunette long enough for Kimberly and Matthew to regain their self-control.

The three of them wrestled their prey onto her back. Kimberly jammed the point of the stake into place and Matthew took the mallet, drove it home with six or seven murderous blows. Blood geysered over them all.

"Not great," Donetta panted, licking blood from her lips. She surveyed the others' wounds and gestured. "But I've seen worse."

"When?" Matthew moaned. Direct

pressure sealed the gashed vein in his neck and his ragged ear slowed to a steady ooze on its own, but the cracked ribs made breathing agony. And the post-rumble blues, just settling on him as his body receded from battle-frenzy, was a most unpleasant surprise.

"My first hunt," Donetta admitted. "I nearly died."

They stared at her in disbelief.

"That's right, and you'd better remember it! We don't age and we heal like nobody's business. But if we're torn up bad enough and can't get food to fuel our recovery, we can still die. We can starve, too, though that shouldn't be a prob—"

Police sirens began to shriek. Still distant, but approaching from more than one direction.

"Into the sewers with 'em, so we can dine in peace."

"What about him?" Matthew indicated the lifeless kid. Latino, thirteen, maybe fourteen.

"Him, too." There was no hesitation in Donetta's voice. "Come on, Matt! Help Kim drag him to that manhole!"

"I won't eat *human* flesh."

"Fine. But we can't leave him. It's our survival, much as the damned vampires. So get your ass moving, now!"

MATTHEW BEZEK sat alone and watched the sunrise from another of the city's abandoned buildings. Two others joined him, about an hour later.

"I'll never get used to this," he said.

Kimberly stroked his elbow. Her other arm was crudely bandaged and several facial scratches were already partially healed. With plenty of fresh meat as a restorative, she'd be back to full-strength in a few days. Ready to Hunt again.

He tossed her a surly glance, refusing to show his relief. "You did it, didn't you? Tell me, which tastes better—vampire flesh or human?"

Kimberly didn't react or withdraw her hand. "No real difference," she told him slowly.

Sickened and unsurprised, Matthew quivered.

"It would've been wrong. Like a sin, Matt. To let it go to waste."

"A sin!" Matthew began to jump up, but his wounds ached too much. He drew a ragged breath. "Okay, Donetta. You've won her over, all the way. You and my Dad, pity you never met! Would've understood each other perfectly. Taught me all this bullshit—about the balance of nature, managing populations. All that shit..."

"And did you hate him for that?"

"No." Out of nowhere, Matthew was crying. "I only hated him for leaving, for dying too damned soon!"

He let Kimberly embrace him gently, no matter how much his ribs ached. He allowed her chin to rest on his shoulder.

Donetta settled to his other side, put down the package she held and touched blunt fingers to his face. The corners of her mouth curled faintly. Her eyes seemed moist, but no tears were allowed to escape.

"Me and Kim ain't goin' nowhere, Matthew. Not for a good long time."

Donetta unwrapped the package. "Best organ meats, Matt. What you need, for your body to regenerate."

"Balance of nature," Matthew grumbled. Then he swallowed, stared. "Is it...?"

"The blonde's heart; her partner's liver and pancreas." She looked deep into Matthew's eyes, daring him to call her a liar. "Just have to trust us, white boy."

Matthew Bezek took a slice of raw flesh and began to chew. ∎

The People of the Wind and Sand

by B. J. Thrower

They had swept round and round the orb of the planet until they achieved self-awareness. They felt emotion, and dreamed of vivid greens while they flowed. They had no time sense, no culture, yet they lived in a perpetual state of ecstatic contentment—a harmonious, harmless, joyous evolution. And the green, the bountiful sand which they ate had never changed.

But insidiously the green became denser, wetter, losing its vitality and flavor. Now it lacked many of the raw biological and mineral ingredients they thrived on. They were forced to dive deeper underground in search of the purer green they required in order to survive. While they fed, they listened apprehensively to the searing heart of the planet, for they had a healthy fear of fire.

They discovered something worse when they breached the surface of the green to fly in the free sky. A new alien presence thwarted them, pressed upon them and prevented the flowing, which is what they *did.* They could sense times of no-pressing, and once, some launched themselves at the stars to destroy the source of the presence, soaring so high above the sand they were lost from the grip of the world. Those who remained retreated into the green but found no solace there, as the sand became increasingly inhospitable and indigestible.

They learned defeat. For the first time in their existence they perceived death. They would not-flow, when they had always flowed. They were alarmed and afraid and then enraged, although rage was as foreign to them as the taste of the poisoned green. The elemental creatures they once were became more emotionally complex, devious and dispassionate.

Their level of intelligence had always suited them and their life circumstance, yet with it they had been unable to make the connection between the havoc being wreaked upon them and the others, whose arrival they had hardly noticed nor now remembered. They might have turned inward and torn themselves asunder——except for her.

They understood that she was female, for they, too, at rare moments mated with two sexes, creating as they flowed. But she was not of the green. They weren't interested in any of the strangers, solid like mud, who were nesting on that single patch of the green on the entire planet of green. But one day she came flowing, a continuous, beating noise that was as similar to flowing as they had ever heard from any solid like mud.

She stopped her peculiar flowing motion nearby. Then in a deliberate, provocative manner she touched the green, making a friction which caused it to glow in such distinctive, intriguing patterns that they instantly and irreversibly made contact.

Gradually, they learned from her who the enemy was. All things solid like mud were the enemy. She was the enemy.

THE GIRL lived in a land covered by a fine silt of green sand. On a "downweather" afternoon, scheduled to be windless, she cartwheeled across the sand attempting to set a new record for herself. Her body flipped rhythmically, drumming, sky and sand indistinguishable blurs. At number forty cartwheel her left wrist failed and she lost her balance, sprawling into the green cushion of the ground.

Forty! Ha-ha, Ernie, you said I couldn't do-o it! Breathless but triumphant in the quiet solitude, she slumped cheerfully over her athletic legs, pretty face flushed, blonde hair braided with bows of sweat and ribbons of sand.

While resting, she admired the sense of space the view provided. Except for the needle towers of the atmosphere processors, she was out of sight of the prefabs where she and three hundred other Pioneers lived, the only people on this planet. She hadn't been born here, yet it was the only place in her memory.

The weight of the land did not intimidate her. She was accustomed to the vast, silent oppressiveness of her home and was perfectly content here.

She contemplated the sand, it greened by microorganisms. The Pioneers had altered the biology of the sand dwellers to make the land susceptible to wide-scale agricultural production, which would accommodate planned-for, planet-wide human colonization. The sand had undergone a lengthy process called "washing," which stripped the topsoil of acidic chemical elements. Washing was accomplished by a combination of infrared scouring and uncommon weather conditions induced from special satellites the Pioneers controlled from the ground.

The girl traced her name idly in the green sand, BRIANNA.

"Yep, that's *moi.*" She giggled, feeling carefree, like she might live forever, always be this happy.

A reed of wind passed diagonally over her shoulder across the bodice of her blue denim jumpsuit. It started to rotate on the sand, forming a small slender funnel one meter tall.

Thrilled, she exclaimed, "It's a baby tornado!" The weather was stable now, tamed and predictable during down-weather days, but Brianna knew that tornadoes had once been an acute problem on Green Planet before the Pioneer terraforming.

The funnel danced for her, swirling and flashing with traces of lime-green luminescence. It whirled into a position above her name, and crudely copied each letter as if an invisible, illiterate hand held the pencil of wind. Watching it in a trance, her jaw dropped.

This phenomenon suddenly struck her with fear. Panic-stricken, she scooted backwards kicking up lumps of sand. She stopped twenty feet away, too startled to even consider running. *Am I dreaming?*

She received an undeniable, fleeting impression of being watched, yet no physical eyes were apparent in the tiny funnel. At the beginning of the shallow ditch her rump had marked through the sand, it waited. There it was, plainly written, another BRIANNA!

During the next year, thirteen-year-old Brianna Brinkley wandered off from the Pioneer Enclave in her spare time, and often the small wind visited her. She wasn't really conscious of the importance of what she was doing, of what she had accomplished by teaching it to imitate her in the rudimentary method of sand writing. She began with the basic English alphabet then progressed to simple nouns: GIRL, SAND, SKY; to verbs, JUMP, HOP, SKIP; and on to sentences. She never knew if the funnel understood the words the letters made, and didn't care. What worried her was whether or not she should reveal this strange game to anyone else. If she did, they might laugh at her, call her a lying butthead. Consequently, she didn't tell a soul, not her parents or her best friend Ernie Ross—and it was a mistake.

THE METEOROLOGY staff was prevented from constantly maintaining the electronic downweather shield, because it caused a machinery overload and power disruption to essential Enclave systems. But they were unable to explain the recent, almost rebellious surges of bad weather during non-downweather periods. These new-phase storms contained windblown ice from the polar caps so deadly, two luckless people caught outdoors had been decapitated. Motion sensors were planted in a five-kilometer radius around the settlement to supplement the weather-tracking satellites, which were vulnerable to cloud cover. But the storms continued to strike with little or no warning, with no discernible pattern or cause.

Brianna squirmed as the Enclave Administrator, Luther Mathias, shoved his narrow gremlin's chin up at her father and growled, "*Abandon* the planet? That's completely out of the question, Brinkley! We've worked too hard. Wear your managerial hat for a moment. *Money's* been invested in us, a great deal of other people's *money!*"

Dr. Ron Brinkley, Chief Meteorologist, looked like he tried to restrain his temper. "Much more than money or our efforts here are at stake now, Luther. We're all in danger——"

Mathias threw out his arms in a gesture of dismissal. "We're Pioneers, for Pete's sake! Danger is the name of this business!" His allies scattered through the community meeting voiced affirmative grunts, bobbed their heads.

Glaring at the brownnosers Ron said, "Nevertheless, the situation is deteriorating. Soon it will be untenable."

Turning to the restless crowd, Mathias exclaimed, "Do you *really* want to be the first Pioneers in history to admit defeat—to run?"

Exasperated, Ron declared, "Do they want to be the first Pioneers to perish wholesale? And just what the hell are you implying by 'managerial hat'? Need I remind you why you hired me? I'm the weather expert here. Mathias, by ignoring me and encouraging others to ignore me you're risking our lives—including our children's."

Mathias sneered, "Aren't you being melodramatic, Ron? I think you're just trying to make excuses for your lack of scientific competency."

Brianna saw her father's face darken with an emotion she couldn't identify. He said, "We measured the speeds, directions and cycles of the jet streams, but we never physically introduced the native wind into the enviromental biome lab. Don't you see that these storms contain a mysterious element, that the wind seems to be exhibiting emotional perception—?"

"Wind like what? Be realistic, Brinkley!" Mathias interrupted with a smirk, as if Brianna's dad had just done him a favor. "We've been here for eleven years, and the only particles of living native tissue we've discovered are the sand bugs, and they're not intelligent. *We* are the sentient life on Green Planet, it's why we were allowed to terraform here to begin with."

"Listen to the man, Mathias," drawled the Chief Enclave Physician Rick Shelton. "We're only human, we may have missed something."

"I won't listen," Mathias said scornfully," and neither should anyone else. This is our home and we're not leaving!"

Ron snapped, "You're suffering from malignant stupidity, or you would have contacted Colony Administration already!"

The meeting erupted with shouts. People were jostled. Everybody had an opinion and nobody listened to anyone else. Young Dr. Shelton waded through the throng and caught Luther Mathias' fist as it swung crookedly at Ron Brinkley.

Brianna, small and forgotten, heard her mother Mary groan in distress. She wanted to tell them about the small wind, but watching their hate-filled, combative faces knew they wouldn't pay attention to her. She was just a kid, and saavy enough to realize that being Ron Brinkley's kid wouldn't help.

When the inconclusive meeting broke up, Ron waved to his daughter with a wan smile. Outside the night was stark and starry, not a downweather night. He had exercised his limited authority and placed the Enclave on high alert status. Not a man who expected others to perform tasks for him, Ron was on duty in the meteorology lab until midnight.

Later Brianna lay wide awake in her wall bunk, missing him. Currently incommunicado with the tiny vortex since Mary was afraid for her to leave the settlement, she knew she should tell dad about her unusual friend. Oh, she didn't want Mr. Mathias to point an accusing finger at her, too. But—in the morning, she decided, she'd finally tell dad everything. It was a relief the long wrestle with her childish conscience was over. She wished she'd been able to make up her mind sooner.

Click-click. The familiar noise drew her troubled attention across the sleeping cubicle to her plas bookcase. The witch had come out of the gingerbread house.

It was the antique weather barometer her father had lovingly brought from Earth and given to her when she was born in transit; which of course she didn't remember, but she treasured it. It was a model based on the fairy tale of "Hansel and Gretel." When the weather was mild, the children stood outside the colorful candy cottage in their quaint, old-European outfits. When barometric pressure dropped the witch popped out, moving the childish figurines into the cottage on a circular track.

Brianna quickly swung off the bunk and padded over the cool steel floor in her bare feet. The door slid open.

Her mother was flopped on the living room sofa, and with a grim expression massaged her temples. Brianna said tentatively, "Mom? The witch just came out of the cottage."

Mary Brinkley sighed. "Brianna, don't you think the gingerbread house is a little primitive compared to daddy's equipment? Now you know I've got one of my headaches, so quit bothering me and get back to bed—"

An alarm shrilled out in the corridor. At the same instant, Ron Brinkley hollered on their private wall intercom, "Mary! We're going to be hit by some hellish straight winds! Take Brianna to cover in the interior hall closet, Mary, *move!*"

"Come on, mama!" Brianna shouted.

Mary bolted upright, lunging off the couch. "Ron! Ron?"

A rattling deluge of hissing sand erupted against the outside wall of the prefab. The colony turbines tripped and the lights blinked ominously. The braying alarm was suddenly smothered by wind that roared like a thousand faceless spirits. The buildings shuddered with a tremendous groan of steel.

Brianna ran toward the closet with Mary on her heels. To her amazement, the floor of the cubicle tilted crazily. She was thrown violently off her feet and rolled shrieking toward the end of the room. It *hurt* when she landed at the bottom of the living room with her mother on top of her. But she understood that the fierce, malevolent wind had actually picked up the building for a moment.

Crumpled inertly in a corner beneath her thrashing mother, Brianna saw green, luminescent-streaked dust explode through the twisted metal of the corridor entrance. She gagged on the cloud, sneezing between half-choked sobs.

The sofa careened weirdly down the slope of the room. Mary helplessly put out her arms and legs to fend it off while the roof tore away with a wrenching *scree-ch*! The sofa became airborne, sucked up in the maelstrom with the rest of the loose furniture as if plucked from the cubicle's skin.

They clung to each other in mindless terror, praying for it to end. For a few seconds the wind seemed to soften, and they heard the horrible screams of wounded people crushed beneath toppled metal walls, echoing all over the Enclave like the cries of birds. The room plunged into darness, except for the greenish glow of the dust envelope.

Then above her mother in the void where the ceiling had been, Brianna saw an immense vortex of green wind. It loomed overhead, bending like a sapling. A separate arm of whistling wind came down at them. Her mother was ripped cruelly from her grasp. Brianna watched Mary's body being flung away into the sinister bleching dust, suspended for one eternal moment with her ankles locked and her arms splayed out as if she were being crucified on the air.

Within the howl of the primeval wind Brianna screamed, "*Mother! Mother! Mother!*" But her pleading cries made no difference—her mother was gone forever. Then the arm of wind returned, and scooped her up, too...

Brianna Brinkley floated on a surreal pillow of turbulent air. Crackling, green bolts of lightning sliced the sullen atmosphere around her like sizzling fireworks. She drifted directly over the crippled Enclave.

A few emergency lighting systems were still operational, denting the preternatural storm-gloom like haphazard, slanted searchlight beams. Half of the buildings were flattened. Steel walls had burst open and resembled silver flower petals, the steel frozen in curls as if it had felt agony.

The towers of the atmosphere processors were erect, but without power were like the fossilized remains of limbless trees. All of the two hundred meter-long biomes used to simulate the environment of Green Planet for terraforming experiments, or containing ecosystems brought from Earth were destroyed, in scattered pyramids of sparkling glass. The row of microwave and transmitting dishes, including the transponder link to Colony Administration were warped to the ground as if they were flat-headed dinosaurs drinking from a polluted, green river.

She watched a bleating goat leap into the black mouth of darkness. An ordinary barnyard hen flapped in her face but it was a corpse of jagged feathers, swept away inside the whirlwind along with her own stolen cry.

Brianna hung in the sand-whipped air, a lost rag doll. She was distantly aware of the grumbling wind. She accepted the fact that she was a hundred feet up in the sky, but that somehow, that she wasn't falling. She knew it should be impossible, she had learned about gravity at Enclave School and yet—it was truly happening. The Pioneer settlement dwindled to a dim shimmer on the horizon.

She was eventually deposited rather gently on the sandy ground. There were other Enclave children lying in limp bundles around her, and she knew on an instinctual level they were alive. She stood swaying and trembling before the cathedral of the vortex which had carried her here.

It rotated in front of her, a majestic citadel of green wind and sand, silent except for its circling, muttering curtains of air. To her shock, it was a lovely thing to behold: Twinkling shades of effervescent greens, with a fiery energy perhaps waxing and waning in visible thought; a hovering beauty of alien evolution; an idea that lived at the bottom of a pleasant well of yearning dreams . . .

The galaxy sprinkled over the vortex as it normally did, stars cold, brilliant white, yet Brianna knew nothing could ever by the same again. She weakly raised her bruised arm, clenching a small defiant fist at the killer of her mother; understanding that her oddball little friend—the small wind—was in some way part of this monstrous thing.

"No," Brianna said, her spoken word pathetic, meaningless. She shook her fist for emphasis, though her arm felt very heavy.

Someone clutched the hem of her pink flannel nightgown. She looked down studidly and saw her best friend and sometimes boyfriend, Ernie Ross. In the eerie green light cast by the vortex, she noticed a bloody gash across his forehead, that he was only wearing underwear. He tugged again. She collapsed.

With an obscene suck of sand the vortex disappeared into the sinking cradle of the earth. A deep, overwhelming silence reigned; windless, odorless, colorless, hopeless.

Grimacing in pain Ernie gathered her against himself, or maybe Brianna gathered him. His lips moved against her ear, his whisper clear and vibrant as church bells, "The wind's alive!" Though she had never personally heard church bells

she imagined that's how they must sound; like Ernie's voice pealing inside her dizzy mind. Tolling the truth, that Brianna had known the wind was alive for a long time.

Then her own personal darkness claimed her. She could stand no more this night.

THE THIRTY Pioneer children woke to a place grown up from the plain like a weed, sudden and thorny, gaudy and pestilant. It appeared to be fashioned from parts of the Enclave, with a half-dozen lopsided, steel and wood buildings. Green neon-like signs hung suspended in the open spaces of empty windows; SOLID LIKE MUD, SAND GIRL, ABCDEFG.

While the youngest children wailed, Ernie stood up and slapped at his sandy thighs. He was dark-haired, dark-eyed, fourteen and a half, dressed in purple jockey shorts. She and Ernie were the oldest, and Brianna's heart sank. What an awesome responsibility it was going to be caring for the other children!

Ernie hollered at the dull sky, "You ain't keeping us in the freak zone!"

In the pale dawn light he marched down the strange street. Brianna thought he looked noble, like a gallant young Indian warrior. When he crossed to the middle of the street beyond the last building, he halted. He could go no further, and she felt a sorrowful surprise that she wasn't surprised at all.

He braced his feet, shoving his shoulders against an invisible barrier. She heard the snap of static, but artificially placed. Ernie made an impulsive charge and bounced off it. He landed on his butt in a puff of green dust. His sleepy, traumatized audience took this slapstick scene in soberly.

Hastily, Brianna persuaded the next two eldest, eleven-year-olds, to herd the rest of the group into a nearby building, although its crazed architecture made it resemble a lunatic asylum. Snatching up fussy babies and heartbroken toddlers, Damon asked cautiously, "What's happening, Brianna?"

"I'm not sure," she replied. A confession laced with dread, because in her case it might be a lie. "I need to talk with Ernie alone, Damon. Hey, I appreciate your help."

"I'll see if there's any water inside," Damon remarked, hoisting three-year-old Twyla to his shoulders for a ride. Twyla had surrendered to the inevitable, and loudly, wetly sucked her thumb. She clutched a thatch of Damon's blonde hair tightly in her free hand.

"Mama? Mama?" she asked over her soggy thumb, with hiccups.

Patting her, Brianna complimented Damon, "Good idea." She felt grateful that from necessity, Pioneer children had more basic survival training than their peers elsewhere.

Damon's blue eyes glistened with emotional bewilderment. "I think my folks were killed last night, Brianna!"

Shakily, she whispered, "Mine, too. T-take them inside."

Ernie gnawed his lower lip, surveying the tempting gap between the buildings. The crooked cut on his forehead had shriveled in a bandage of dried blood. Worried, Brianna said, "It's a good thing you've got a thick skull. You okay?"

He hooted, "Yeah! Never been better!" His rich dark eyes smoldering as he stared up at her. "I guess this is some kind of goofy prison."

"It might be a prison, but it's not goofy." She dropped gracefully to her knees in the lane of sand. Selecting words carefully, she wrote on it. The calm sunshine dappled her mussed hair to gold. a seam of bedraggled pink lace drooped from the bodice of her dirty nightgown. Her pearly hands stroked the sand as if she were finger painting; fingertips creating the friction which defined her letters so well for alien eyes.

Ernie read aloud, "'Small wind, where are you?' What's that mea——"

The vortex punched up out of the ground with a blast-like roar of sand-filled wind. They stumbled to their feet, quaking in fear. A greenish-white finger of light penetrated the area of the forcefield, bringing the charred smell of ozone. It zapped the sand beside Brianna's message, spelling BURY THEM. Obviously, she had been an excellent teacher.

Petrified but determined, she untangled herself from Ernie, sinking to her knees again. She wrote, NO THIS IS WRONG.

Sparking with menace, the wind-finger underlined its brief statement. Brianna did the same to hers, turning to stare at the huge sentinel of air and trying to assume a stern countenance. Having observed the interplay between them, she heard Ernie gasp with delayed reaction.

Wondering if he would despise her now, Brianna scribbled, IT IS WRONG FOR YOU TO BURY THEM, MEAN AND HATEFUL TO BRING US HERE!!!

The chilling reply: THEY YOU CHANGED THE GREEN, THEY YOU CHANGED US, ALL THINGS SOLID LIKE MUD WILL BE BURIED.

"'Solid like mud'?" Ernie said, teeth chattering.

She thought about it, then told him, "Us. The Enclave."

In her immature, inadequate way, Brianna had wondered if the decade of terraforming preceding total colonization had hurt the people of the wind and sand, if that's why the small wind had approached her, although it'd never offered an explanation. The secret she'd kept so close to her heart, perhaps jealously, while everything rotted.

She crabwalked sideways, writing around Ernie's foot. WE ARE NOT SOLID LIKE MUD. WE ARE HUMAN BEINGS. WE DID NOT KNOW WE HURT YOU, MAYBE WE CAN STOP AND YOU STOP TOO.

WE WILL BURY YOU; burned on the sand with a tombstone finality. And that was the lesson for today, she supposed, because the vortex vanished into its green cocoon leaving only a remnant breeze to trickle through her hair, and perhaps to watch them? *Who was teaching whom now?*

Bunching his fists, Ernie shrieked, "You killed my big brother, you bastards!" He leapt at the forcefield, clawed it, but it only repelled him. He tumbled to the ground again, topsy-turvey, a clumsy acrobat.

Brianna helped him up. He glared. Her cheeks flamed—she hung her head in shame. He yelled, "You knew about them!"

She nodded. A tear traveled down her grubby cheek.

"You should have told! Why didn't you tell, Brianna! Why didn't you tell me?" He was livid and now he shoved her, just a little, but she didn't fall.

She wept, feeling as if she would die from the suffocating burden of guilt. "I—was going to tell my dad this morning! I—didn't want everyone to think I was crazy! Who would've listened to me?" she said, knowing Ernie would have. He was terribly angry with her, her judge, her jury, at last.

She pleaded, not for forgiveness but for his understanding, babbling, "Ernie, it was a tiny friendly wind, it was cute, never that big monster, I didn't know about that, and it never, *ever* answered me before, it only copied me! It was a game, I swear it! I swear." She waited there in her tattered pink nightgown before the furious, tanned boy in his undershorts.

After awhile, he simply clasped her hand and led her back along the street; of all things she least expected he decided to offer compassion. She was so grateful she cried even harder.

Five-year-old Chuckie Wong sat upon the mostly wooden porch of the ramshackle building, swinging his pj-clad legs over the edge super-duper fast. He munched on an apple from one of the Enclave agricultural biomes.

Brianna sniffling beside him, Ernie demanded, "Where'd you get that, Chuckie?" Solemnly the little fellow pointed at the door where Damon appeared, grinning at them.

He said, "There's a whole room with boxes of food and jugs of water. Lucky, huh?"

"Lucky," Ernie grunted.

"Whooo. Whoo-whoo," Chuckie said mysteriously. Apple juice dripped off his chin.

"Very good, Chuck," Ernie said somberly. To her, "They want to keep us alive?"

"Until they bury us," Brianna agreed.

A mystified frown. "Why, Brianna? They're your buddies."

"No, they're not! I don't know why," Brianna replied in honest misery. "I—I'm hungry," she added feebly, as if it were something to be embarrassed about. So they climbed the steps together, and went indoors to find some breakfast.

"Dat jy-ant in da wind said 'whoo-whoo' to Ernie and Brianna," remarked Chuckie Wong on the porch in the freak zone. "Whooooo."

NO! GO away!" Ernie signaled the Enclave crew in the approaching hoverdozer by making exaggerated negative gestures with his arms and head. "Stay back!"

"Pleasepleaseplease," Brianna chanted, poised on her tiptoes beside him, nose nearly in the tingle of the forcefield.

Ernie screamed at the vehicle, "You'll be wind-killed! You morons, listen to me!"

A resolute adult voice projected from the dozer's p.a. system, "Is that Ernie Ross? Hang on! We're digging you kids out this time."

Ernie stared at her. "They're all crazy. They've flipped!"

Brianna shook her head, numbed at the prospect of yet another doomed rescue mission launched by the survivors from the Enclave. Cramping, her toes dug into the sand feeling for the coming of the sentinel. Dread parched her throat dry.

The dozer banked neatly at the forcefield, extended air jets fanning up a green geyser of sand as it settled on its powerful treads. The air jets shut down, and the crew immediately deployed the huge dish of the scoop. Ernie raced along the border of the forcefield as the scoop bit the earth with a heavy *thud.* With a hydraulic whine it lifted the load of sand and dumped it behind the ten-ton body of the vehicle.

Ernie pointed maniacally at the trench. "That's your grave, man! Your graves!"

The booming, condescending male voice from the dozer cabin, "Yes, we're digging you out, Ernie."

Under her bare feet Brianna felt the vibration of the shock wave rising through the subterranean sand. "Ernie—"

"*It's coming!*" he shrieked.

Brianna caught a glimpse of the dozer operator's face, a white smudge with dark spots of terrified eyes; Mr. Staleovich, the Maintenance Chief. Luther Mathias was tapping the upper echelons of his dwindling staff for "troops" now. She turned away and dropped, plunging her hands in the sand. NO! NOT AGAIN. PLEASE LET THEM GO!

The sentinel rose above the surface with a deafening tornadic roar. Brianna refused to watch. She lay stretched out on her stomach, hand moving drearily, NO NO NO...

She heard the staccato firing of several ineffective laser pulse rifles. Strangled cries echoed from the dozer's loudspeakers, mercifully brief. Then the great bellowing of the wind washed all other sound away.

As the rumbling underground gradually diminished, Ernie walked over. She quit writing, rolling listlessly on her back.

"Got those dumb suckers," he said. "Took 'em down in the cold, hard ground. R. I. P. Here lies more stupid—"

"Shut up!" she cried.

He mused, "How many times will we have to see that?"

Until they quit trying to save us, or until it kills all of them, Brianna thought, depressed. *And when it doesn't need us for bait anymore, then it'll kill us.*

The vortex came up, flinging odds and ends over the top of the forcefield; a pair of lightly bloodied work gloves, a thermos of hot coffee, a ruler. Sick with failure, she stumbled away.

Wind-finger wandering, the vortex wrote BURIED THEM.

Glancing at the message in disinterest, Ernie said, "Well, you sure as shit did. Whoopee-do for you."

After waiting fruitlessly for a response, the sentinel folded into itself and went underground. Deathly quiet touched the Zone—as it had become coloquially known—like ghostly hands.

The rest of the kids streamed out from cover to scavenge. Ernie joined them, but the junk bored him. He'd long ago appropriated clothes, a pocket knife, even a quaint compass. Things appeared in here in random, idiotic ways, sort of like the adult Pioneers appeared just outside the Zone.

The older children assumed that——like the Zone—the Enclave was being dealt with by slow burial. After the devastating attack the night they were taken the storms blew in lazily, once or twice a week, in a natural unintellectual pattern. The people of the wind and sand were apparently free to resume their destiny unhindered. Brianna held many sand conversations with the Zone sentinel as the weeks then months passed by, but communications lessened with the number of rescue attempts.

From the flat roof of their primary Zone house, to which they climbed on a ladder thrown in by the sentinel, the short horizon once again revealed the nacreous dome of the sky pinched against the brooding land. The green-black smudge signal of another sand storm brewed beyond the Zone.

On that particular day, much like all the other days, Ernie concluded, "They're all b-u-r-i-e-d. I guess that makes us the Pioneers now." He whistled like a descending rocket. "Looks like we're in for another big blow, Pioneers. Let's get ready for it. Don't worry, squirtlings, they'll sent a shuttle from Colony Administration—really, they will."

TIME STOOD still. Ernie confided in Brianna his concern about their dwindling food and water supplies. But she didn't know how to answer him, consumed in her terrible guilt. Little Twyla woke them every night bawling from nightmares, and Brianna was likewise troubled by a potent dream.

Genuine bells rang and chimed. She was safely out of the Zone and living on Earth, a mature, proud woman at her wedding. Radiant, she walked down a flower-strewn aisle, saw Ron and Mary smiling at her and noticed that her guests were the lost Pioneers from Green Planet —but this was a wonderful thing and she was overjoyed to see them again. She thought Ernie was her groom, but when she stepped up to the Pioneer Leader Luther Mathias, who was officiating, the dark vortex exploded through the white floor of the peaceful church. Looking up the tall column she understood she was to marry *it*, as the ultimate punishment for her silence.

Her beautiful satin wedding dress became the torn nightgown she had worn in the Zone. The shining medals around her neck which she'd won as a professional gymnast, disappeared. Luther Mathias transformed into a demon with toadstool ears, thrusting a prehistoric purple and yellow-spotted tongue at her, screaming,

"Say I do, Brianna! *Say I do!*"

She would awaken to another crushing onslaught of grief and remorse. Sometimes she considered killing herself, but didn't because, for now, the little ones needed her.

Ernie sensed when her despair was bleakest. He tried to encourage her by talking about the future, or the shuttle. But it was very tough to feel any hope now. When Ernie became moody she consoled him, occasionally with her body in the mellow stuffiness of the dusty house, where they would lie together among the remaining plastic jugs of tepid water and receive the brief stabbing pleasure from the other.

As parental substitutes, Brianna and Ernie had learned by trial and error to enforce a group siesta every afternoon. On the roof under a boring azure sky one warm day, Chuckie sat up and said, "Sea gull! Jonathan Livingston Seagull!" Brianna had been reciting the story to them from memory.

Drowsy, she murmured, "Not now, Chuck. Be good."

"He's flyin', mama," he insisted. "Fly faster, Jonathan!"

Ernie scrambled up in time to catch the arrow of a long range shuttle streak across the bowl of the sky. Simultaneously, the vortex rose at the entrance of the Zone.

Brianna darted down the rattletrap ladder leaning on the outside of the house, since a gradual thick tide of sand had flooded the front porch and blocked the door there. Snatching for her and missing, Ernie shouted at Damon, "Let's hide the kids inside the house, hurry!" Helping Damon hoist the ladder through a hole in the roof, Ernie called after her, "Dammit, Brianna, wait!"

She ran to the edge of the forcefield, kneeling in the green and bowing her trembling golden head. The greenish light of it strangely subdued, the vortex sent its separate arm through the forcefield to her. Oddly, the finger of wind touched her hair before it dropped to the sand. WHAT IS IT?

A STARSHIP WITH OTHER HUMANS.

ALL THINGS SOLID LIKE MUD ARE BURIED OR ARE IN THE ZONE.

Brianna rocked on her kees in concentration, struggling to grasp something *significant* in that last sentence—

Having flung himself off the roof to a sand dune, Ernie arrived at a gallop. Scanning the messages, he hollered in excitement, "They don't know there're more of us!"

"Yes!" Her fingers flew, and Ernie wondered if she was writing on the surface of their minds. THERE ARE AS MANY HUMANS AS THERE ARE STARS. MORE HUMANS WILL COME, AND THEY WILL KEEP COMING UNTIL THEY UNDERSTAND WHO YOU ARE AND WHAT YOU HAVE DONE HERE.

The appendage curled backwards into the rampart of itself, as if rendered "speechless" by this revelation.

Ernie cried, "The Colonial Rangers, the Ranger Engineering Corps! Tell them how they'll burn this world to ashes when they find out! To ashes, you goblins, you green farts—ka-POW! Rangers burn hostile life forms like you!" She did write it, since it was the truth. It had happened before.

The vortex advanced, interrupting the forcefield in a shower of sparks, a million billion hot blue diamonds. The air became supercharged with static electricity.

Brianna dimly shrieked. In the bellow of the wind-thing Ernie couldn't hear her, yet her lips said RUN ERNIE! But he couldn't, wouldn't leave her. His hair literally stood on end.

The arm of wind struck him powerfully in the chest and his breath punched out. The unseen giant in the wind bent Ernie over in a reluctant bow, then ruthlessly crushed his face in the deep coffin of sand. Smothering, he was vaguely aware that Brianna was tugging on him, but he knew she didn't have the strenght to save him. With a final convulsion, he relaxed. Then the finger of wind flipped him on his aching back while Brianna was blown away like a tumbleweed.

The funnel cloud leaned over him like a sorcerer's vision.

Caked sand in his mouth, grainy under his tongue, crammed up his nostrils, Ernie moaned, "No! I don't wanna die!"

She crawled doggedly toward him, fighting the horrible power of the wind with only her will and her tired adolescent muscles. It was her wedding day, Brianna knew it now, with a bitter harvest of residue in her dry mouth. *Come so soon, come too soon* . . . She pledged her marriage vows, not the words Luther Mathias urged her to speak in her dream but, "No, Ernie doesn't want to die!" Her bulging emerald eyes gazed up and up the tower of it.

The last thing Ernie Ross felt was the stinging rain of sand pellets on his cheeks. The last thing he saw were his poor legs being methodically covered by the relentless sand, shoveled by the mean, green wind . . . *Bury me* . . .

Drawn to the Zone by its fluctuating energy emissions, the shuttle loomed overhead with the shape of a great pale vulture. Sleek snub nose up, wings dipping at a slight pitch and yaw, engines droning, the shuttle made its sweeping pass with precision, but much too slowly, Brianna knew.

Beyond the Zone, a spinning living forest. They launched themselves at the shuttle, wind-birds of prey. Engulfed within the green void of the Zone sentinel she heard the distant thunder and boom of the shuttle boosters, as the command crew attempted a jarring, rapid ascent to escape from the vast battalion of charging tornadoes.

WE FLOW, they told her.

She floated upside down in the billowing amniotic mist. A sensuous green light raced along her arms, displaying her throbbing veins as jeweled threads—green light pumping like her body's blood. She welcomed it. Strange to feel glad. Dozens of trianges of luminescent green eyes gazed upon her. Their racial memories filled her soul and purged her guilt forever . . .

Later, wearing a glowing crown of green sand she was lifted to the summit of the sentinel, riding it like a misted chariot out to the site of the flaming shuttle wreck, where they found a lone survivor.

FROM THE other side of the locked door in the Enclave, Damon's voice was shrill with terror, "Go away, Brianna! Leave us *alone!*"

"Damon," she said patiently. "Damon, don't be a butthead. You don't have to be afraid of me. I won't hurt you."

She knew her voice was different now, *gritty.* She had seen her reflection, but she thought she looked, well, breathtaking. She was encased in a shining skin of green light. Her hair had become a thickened sprinkle of sparkling delicate sand which flowed off her head in a gentle stream. Her arms melded into the aura since she wouldn't need them any more. Sand swam in the corneas of her eyes.

"Where's Ernie?" Damon screamed. "We want Ernie!"

"I told you he's in the infirmary. He's going to be fine, but if you want to see him you have to come out," she said kindly. "We'll go see him together."

"No! No—I can't." Damon moaned.

"Well, okay. I'll check on you later. Damon, keep your eye on everyone. Don't forget to change the babies' diapers."

"I—I won't."

It disturbed her a little that Damon feared her now. Brianna drifted down the ravaged corridor toward the battered infirmary. *He'll remember we're friends,* she thought firmly. *He'll come around.*

A short med bot tended to a mass of intravenous tubes in the man's neck and hands; according to the low red lights on the monitor board, a severely injured man. The stranger in the infirmary was dressed in nothing but purple and black bruises, the pile of his clothes the bot had cut off pooled on the floor in melancholy strips. They were still identifiable as the uniform of a command co-pilot, with the Colony Administration insignia stitched on the breast pockets.

"Huh?" Ernie mused groggily, belted on an exam couch with an oxygen tube up his nose. "How the—?" A twilight of green light flickered on the ceiling, preceding her. Ernie stirred.

"Hellow, Ernie." Brianna stepped into view.

Seeing her, he gasped. After a long minute, he cried out, "No! Brianna! What *happened?*"

She smiled tentatively and said, "Now the people of the wind and sand can understand you, and you can understand them, through me. They just took me sand diving! It was wonderful! They pass through the green like you breath, Ernie, they eat the green. I ate the green." She frowned at his expression of horror, but elaborated hopefully, "The shuttle surprised them, Ernie, you were right. They didn't know there were lots more solid like mud, us, er—you, I mean. You're so smart.

"The co-pilot ejected before the shuttle crashed. He told me they sent an emergency message to the Rangers. Don't you understand, Ernie? *I* can talk to the Rangers when they come, no more sand writing or secrets, no more mistakes, no more guilt. Nobody else has to go hungry, or be afraid, or die!" But by his silence, his stunned withdrawal, he hurt her. She exclaimed in frustration, "Are you scared of me, too? Ernie? Are you crying? That's not right, Ernie, I feel so *good* now. I'm happy again. Hey, you're my knight in shining armor, aren't you? I—I love you."

Brianna could have explained that taking a human into themselves was a logical step for the people of the wind and sand, since they didn't want to be burned to ashes by solid like mud as numerous as stars. But that would come later. And it might seem sad to him that she'd sacrificed more than everything because she'd been the secret link to an alien race, she understood that, though she didn't *feel* sad.

But to her relief, because he was a Pioneer, because it was the truth, Ernie finally found the courage and wisdom to answer, "I love you, too, Brianna." ∎

The Domain was Fire.
The Laws.
by Thomas Canfield

Earth, Wind, Water, and Fire. The four points of the compass, the four schemes of creation. Which was this, Talisman wondered. He opened his clenched fist, allowed the fine sand to drift through his fingers. The rolling dunes stretched before him, timeless, pure, without flaw. The sun beat down mercilessly upon the sand, the glare stabbing angrily at Talisman's eyes. He pulled his cowl forward, shielded his eyes. The distant glimmer of horizon revealed nothing.

Talisman bent again, worked his hand

into the sand. His lips parted slightly and he waited, feeling nothing. A numbness gradually crept over his hand, stole up his arm. The sun shifted in the sky. The numbness changed to pain, the flesh of Talisman's arm beginning to prickle and burn—the kiss of the brand. Talisman smiled. It was fire then. The domain was Fire. The laws. He stood up. The sun was already low on the horizon. It burned redly, dusted the sand with crimson. Talisman clutched his staff, strode resolutely into the fierce gale of the sun.

The domain was Fire. The laws.

FIRST LIGHT. Talisman's eyes opened, stared into the purple vault of heaven above. He lay there without moving. He was curled up in the hollow of a wind-sculpted dune, his staff at his side. He sensed that he was being watched. Very carefully he reached out and retrieved his staff. He lay still a moment longer, listening. Then, in one fluid, seamless movement he vaulted to his feet.

There were two of them. One he could make out distinctly, sprinting along the crest of the dune; the long mane of hair down its spine, the great webbed feet beating against the earth. Hajah! How had they managed to sneak up on him?

Talisman raised his staff, inscribed an arc in front of him. A brief flash of light shattered the peaceful dawn. The hajah spun around, then dropped to the sand. It twitched for a moment, then lay still.

The second hajah chattered at him furiously. It slipped behind a row of hillocks, disappeared. Talisman worked his way carefully up the face of the dune. He reached the crest, surveyed the surrounding countryside. A stealthy shadow flitted briefly in the distance, darting from one dune to another. Then there was nothing.

Satisfied, Talisman walked over to the dead hajah. He grasped the mane of hair that ran along its spine, brushed it aside. He studied the intricately wrought tattoo on its neck. The hajah were outriders, chattels of the estate. They patrolled the thousands of acres of sand, seeking out and killing trespassers and poachers. They had a legal right to kill and, under the code, could have killed him. Talisman smiled grimly. Of course he was not obliged to allow himself to be killed.

Talisman turned, looked at the eastern sky. The rim of the sun had pushed up above the horizon, light spilled over the sand. A short distance ahead a road twisted its way among the drifts and dunes. He made his way toward it rapidly. Once on the road, technically, he was no longer on the estate's property, no longer trespassing. They might still attempt to kill him of course. But they would no longer be rooted in certainty, they would hesitate. And Talisman would seize on that moment of hesitation, exploit it.

Talisman made the road at the same moment that three hajah brested a dune off to his left. The hajah danced and gesticulated with indignation. A man came up behind them. He strode surveying the road for a moment, sent one of the hajah on ahead to block Talisman's path. Then he advanced with the other two. Talisman waited calmly for them to approach, holding his staff casually at his side.

The man pushed his way onto the road grimly, positioned himself in front of Talisman. The hajah followed, skipping and stunting in their eagerness to get at Talisman. He paid no attention to them. Everything depended on the man.

"So, grandfather. You have lost your way, perhaps?" the man said, without offering a greeting.

"Not as surely as you have lost yours," Talisman replied. "Where are your manners?" It was very bad form not to offer a greeting. A deliberate mark of disrespect.

"You crossed over our land." The man's arm swept over the endless stretch of sand. "You killed one of our hajah."

"I crossed over no man's land," Talisman maintained stoutly. "Who accuses me of trespassing?" The man frowned. It was of course the hajah who had summoned him and the hajah's accusation carried no weight.

"One of the hajah has been killed. Do you claim you had nothing to do with it?"

"I kill hajah frequently," Talisman spat fiercely. "It gives me pleasure to do so. I will kill these here if they do not behave themselves." The hajah retreated a short distance, hissing and beating their webbed feet against the earth.

"Stop that at once," the man commanded. The hajah kicked fretfully at the earth, subsided. Their red eyes stared at Talisman with a coruscating hatred. "Are you telling me that you mean to destroy my lord's property?" He cast a brief glance at the hajah. "These hajah are his valued servants."

"They are perhaps worth more alive than they they are dead," Talisman allowed. "To your master at least. To say that he values them, however, surely that does him an injustice. They are foul, despicable creatures. Offensive to the sight and to the mind." One of the hajah rose out of its crouch, the mane of hair along its spine erect. A low, snarling noise rumbled in its throat.

Talisman turned on it instantly. He raised his staff and the hajah was engulfed in a shimmering curtain of heat. It struggled for a brief moment, pawing at the air, then disappeared in a mass of flame. It spun across the stone bed of the road seeking to escape and collapsed in a shuddering heap. The flames burned brighter for an instant then finally guttered and went out, great wisps of smoke drifting from the charred corpse.

The man staggered backwards, his expression incredulous and uncomprehending. With an effort he pulled himself together, stepped over to examine the corpse, the second hajah cowering behind him, then turned to Talisman.

"You are of the Seven Orders," he said quietly. "I was not aware of it. Why are you traveling as you are? And what is your Order?"

"I am travelling as I am because I choose to." Talisman's eyes glittered. "My Order is the ancient and esteemed one of the Circle and the Star." The Orders were all ancient. But they were not esteemed so much as they were feared and resented. Talisman knew this but still he observed the formula.

"The Circle and the Star," the man repeated. "I have not seen such a one since I was a youth." He studied Talisman curiously, seemed disappointed. "I do not remember them so. But it was long ago."

"Perhaps it was an elder," Talisman replied, amused. "They have more of grandeur about them."

"Perhaps. We do not see much of the Orders in these parts." The man's eyes rested briefly on Talisman's staff. "Well, grandfather. I won't ask you what your business might be. I do not care to know it. It is not lightly said that the Orders bring trouble in their wake. It was always so. I am willing to see you pass. Even to wish you well. But if you do set foot upon my lord's property we will kill you."

"That would not be easy," Talisman

said lightly. "But I take what you say in good sort. It is plain and forthright. I, for my part, will kill you if I am hindered or delayed further."

The man inclined his head. "As you say, Seeker of Stars." He used the common term. He stepped aside to let Talisman pass, again inclined his head. "May fire touch you."

"The flame shall cleanse," Talisman completed the ritual. He passed on down the road. When he looked back some time later, they were gone. Only the trackless sand over which he had come remained.

DAY FOLLOWED day, week succeeded week. Talisman lost all track of time. Always it was the same. The endless stretch of sand. The sun. The narrow skirting of death. The same until he bent over yet another dead hajah, lifted it by its mane of hair to examine the tattoo. Serpent and sword, crest of fire. Just as he had been told. He let the hajah drop to the ground. The estate must lie east, there, where the sun was coming up. No more than a day's hard journey now.

Talisman stared out over the barren leagues of sand speculatively. The reports that had come back to them, the stories, the rumors, were vague and unsubstantiated. Few could bring themselves to believe that they were true. The heresy, the transgression, was too great. Yet Talisman wondered. Even now, as he stood there, he could sense something of discord. Something of defilement. Could sense . . . He shook his head, unwilling to pursue the thought further. He grasped his staff, started forward.

The sun crept up into the sky. The pale, delicate blue faded, was bleached a searing, uniform white. The molten mass of the sun beat down on Talisman, rose toward its zenith. It was still, unnaturally so. There was a palpable absence of movement, of life. Talisman seemed the lone living entity, the sole focus of regard of the bright, unwinking eye overhead. He did not trust the stillness. He shielded his eyes, fought to penetrate the dazzling, sun-scorched whiteness. Rippling waves of heat shimmered above the sand, distorted distances. He could not gauge how far he had come, how far he had to go.

Suddenly, a lone hajah appeared out of the rippling curtain of heat. Talisman and hajah became aware of the other at the same instant. Both stopped. Both regarded the other with surprise. Then the hajah continued to walk toward him, as though determined to ignore his presence. Odd, Talisman thought warily. Maybe it was stupid from the sun. Hajah usually only patrolled at dawn and at dusk. They did not like the brutal heat of mid day.

The hajah came on blindly; Talisman waited. It passed within thirty feet of him, turned once, looked at him. Its red eyes were dull and glazed, its blunt features devoid of hostility. It showed no inclination to fight. Talisman did not know what to do. He should destroy the hajah, he knew. But he found it difficult to do so without the creature first attacking him. He almost let it pass but . . . the thought remained with him still. The domain was Fire. The law. He raised his staff.

The hajah walked serenely on. Talisman almost willed its destruction . . . then it became clear to him. Of course! The hajah was under a spell. It was a decoy, a feint. A means to gauge the strength of this adversary now approaching—to test his, Talisman's, powers. It was not the hajah's destruction he had almost willed, but his own as well. He lowered the staff.

The hajah continued on its path,

passed on out of sight. Talisman stared after it thoughtfully. It was not an easy thing, to cast a spell on a hajah. To destroy one was nothing, the work of a child. To cast a spell over one required a high order of discipline and focus. The pattern, the range, must mesh exactly. He was not sure that he himself could do it, though he had never tried. That it was a member of the Orders who had done it he now knew was true.

He plunged ahead again, certain that he was almost there. Working his way to the crest of a massive dune he caught his first sight of the fortress; a blunt mass of rock and chiseled carapaces thrust above the surrounding sand, stark and ominous. Talisman stood there a moment without moving, his gaze fixed and unwavering. Then he started down the face of the dune. He might have waited till nightfall, some seven hours off, but the dark was not as effective a cloak as his apparent defenselessness and lack of guile. He could not hope to accomplish his mission by means of force alone. It would take cunning and deception as well. He crossed the last stretch of sand as though weary, reached the base of the wall. He leaned against the great quarried blocks of stone, appeared to rest.

A nonthrall poked its ugly face out over the parapet. "You there," he called angrily. "Vagabond. What do you think you're doing?"

"Sheltering from the sun, kind sir," Talisman said in a weak voice. "Would it be possible to get a drink of water?"

"Water?" The nonthrall glared at him. "What do you imagine this to be, a hostelry? You are on private land. Your life, by rights, is forfeit. There'll be no water for you. Only death."

"I did not come here to seek death," Talisman said patiently. He looked up into the swarthy, misshapen face. "Only respite from the sun."

The nonthrall made an exclamation of annoyance. "Here. Bring this miscreant to me," he said to someone below. "We shall see what it is, that seems not to comprehend the nature of death."

Talisman smiled faintly to himself. He could, of course, have thrown up a field and used it to scale the wall. But this was so much simpler, having them open the gate for him. Three hajah padded around the wall, formed a phalanx behind him. They prodded him along using the butt ends of spears they carried. Talisman ran before them obediently till they came to a narrow opening between two blocks of stone. He was forced to turn sideways to slide through it. the nonthrall waited for him on the other side.

He strutted forward, examined Talisman with a venomous scowl. Dressed in a leather jerkin, the haft of a knife showing at his belt, he was an ugly sight. Squat, burly, with clipped ears and narrow, bloodshot eyes, he seemed a cross between man and beast. Nonthralls, like hajah, were serfs of the estate. But they occupied a more exalted position, serving as overseers of a sort. They were quick to anger, irrascible by nature.

"Show me your face that I might spit in it," the nonthrall addressed Talisman, who was not sure whether this was meant literally or whether it was a form of greeting. Either way he did not much care for it. He threw back his cowl. The nonthrall peered up at him, his mouth twisted in fierce distaste. "You do not look so very terrible," he said mockingly, "for a man who is about to die."

"Enough of that," Talisman said curtly, dropping his facade. "I have business to conduct with your master. You must take me to him."

The nonthrall looked astonished. "The only business you have to do with is the business of death!" he cried at last. He drew his knife from his belt. "I shall kill you myself, to repay you for your insolence."

Talisman glared at him with contempt. Without moving or in any way touching him he slammed the nonthrall against the stone wall. The knife clattered to the ground. "I am not going to repeat myself a second time," Talisman said. "You will take me to your master. Or I will dismember you. Slowly. I would quite enjoy that."

The nonthrall struggled briefly, beat his fists against the stone wall in an effort to escape. "The hajah! Where are my hajah!" he snarled.

Talisman had filled the passageway with pseudo-stone, a mimic structure that would evaporate within the hour. The hajahs were trapped outside. For the moment.

"They are not your hajah, but mine," he taunted the nonthrall. "They have sold you out." The nonthrall struggled mightily. "I will give them to you if you like," Talisman whispered gently. "They mean nothing to me. But first you must cooperate."

The nonthrall clawed at the air. "Give them to me now. I must kill them. I must!"

Talisman considered. "No. Later. You must take me to the great lord, that I might converse with him."

The nonthrall shook his head in terror. "I cannot do that!"

"No, perhaps you can not," Talisman conceded. "The chapel then. Show me the way to the chapel. I shall seek him out on my own."

The nonthrall again struggled to free himself, finally went limp. "Yes. Alright,"

he said at last. A look of cunning had come into his eyes. "I can do that."

Talisman released him and the non- thrall, moving tentatively, beckoned for Talisman to follow him. They crossed a courtyard of hard packed sand, the sand colored and laid out in a pattern of huge interlocking diamonds, black and grey and shale blue. A great mass of black stone reared out of the sand, an archway cut into it. The nonthrall slipped quickly under the arch and began climbing a series of narrow steps. Talisman followed, ready to kill the nonthrall at the first hint of treachery.

The steps were carved into the sheer face of the stone itself. They appeared to be very ancient. Their path branched once, dipping to the left around a fracture in the stone, and then a second time. They emerged into a flat, open space, jagged spires of rock rising up on either side of them. Before them stood a small stone chapel. Blasted and shattered remnants of boulders littered the ground. The sky above was a fiery display of color.

"This is it," the nonthrall announced, laboring for breath. "You must enter the chapel. By moving the altar you will have access to the secret passageway. It will take you to the lord's domain." The nonthrall smiled faintly.

Talisman nodded. He did not trust the nonthrall, could not leave him to roam freely. "Give me your hand," he said. "Place it against the rock. I must have a pledge." The nonthrall hesitated, then placed his hand against the rock. "The other as well." The nonthrall complied, lips twisted faintly in scorn. "Affirm your faith with these words. Trust. Sanctity. Endeavor." The nonthrall repeated the words. Talisman fused the pattern of the stone with that of the hands so that the two became one. "Fine. Be careful that you don't try to move."

The nonthrall became aware that something was wrong. He jerked at his hands without effect. "My hands! What have you done to my hands?" he cried.

"It won't last," Talisman reassured him. "Not beyond tomorrow anyhow. I expect by then you won't be able to do any harm."

"My hands!" the nonthrall wailed, stricken. "You've done something to my hands!"

Talisman walked over to the chapel, entered. It was cool inside, dark. The little light that filtered in was enough only to cast everything into deep shadow. He hesitated. The sense of defilement was here as well, stronger than before. He made his way to the front where the altar stood. He ran his hands lightly over the top seeking a means of moving it. A metal ring set in the stone brushed against his palm. He grasped it, lifted. There was a grating sound as the stone shifted and then the whole altar swung away.

A tunnel led down into the earth. A dank, wet smell of decay emanated from its depths. Talisman peered into the tunnel blindly, straining to detect any sound or movement. There was none. He ventured a few feet into the darkness, feeling his way as he went. The footing was slick underneath, strewn with rubble. The walls oozed moisture. Talisman made his way forward slowly, the descent steep and difficult, seemingly without end.

Suddenly the tunnel widened, broadened. The air became drier. The outer chambers must lie somewhere just up ahead. Light began to filter into the tunnel. Talisman heard noises now, rumblings and hissings, the cries of men. He hugged the wall, slipped forward like a shadow. A great cavern opened out before him, filled with flickering red light that jumped and pulsed against the stone. He stared out on a sickening, nightmarish scene.

Soot-blackened men, thin and spectral, labored over piles of earth and crushed stone. Great cauldrons of liquid metal, hissing and spitting, were drawn along a set of rails, teams of men harnessed to them by cable and rope. Giant nonthralls weilding bullwhips strutted amongst the men, bellowing hoarsely and lashing out without provocation. The domain was Earth. The laws.

Talisman clutched at his head. A tremor wracked his stomach. He sank to his knees, retching. The harsh, ionized air burned at his lungs, the shrill clamour and cries ratcheted through his skull. The two domains, that of Fire and that of Earth. They were seperate, distinct. They could not be joined, could not both hold. Yet Talisman could feel the dissonant impulses racing through his body, filling him with an indelible sense of pollution, of violation. The great Law had been breached, the transgression consumated.

A shadow fell upon Talisman's prostrate form, remained there. Rough hands seized him by the shoulders, dragged him to his feet.

"The pit! The pit! To the pit with him," a voice cried. He was hoisted onto the backs of several nonthralls, borne aloft through the chaos and strife of the quarry. They carried him across a broken, shattered outcropping of rock, jostling him roughly, finally flung him down by a bubbling pit of what looked to be liquid tar. Flames guttered across its surface, died. A bitter, pungent smell filled the air.

"In with him," a nonthrall growled, kicking him in the ribs. "Rid the world of this filth." A bullwhip lashed across his thighs. A second followed. There was a general scramble and then bullwhips fell upon him in a steady torrent, lacerating his flesh, driving him toward the pit. Talisman clutched his staff, felt life receding from him in a blaze of pain and black despair.

"A minute," a voice said softly. The hail of bullwhips ceased. A gaunt, wizened figure bearing a staff shuffled forward. "Ah," he exclaimed with satisfaction. "Circle and Star." He dipped the corner of his robe in the pool of blood at Talisman's feet. His eyes blazed with a fierce relish. "Do you know who I am?" he asked.

Talisman looked up at him. "Serpent," he said through gritted teeth. "Order of the Serpent."

"Yes," the gaunt head bent in acknowledgement. "I am more than that, however. This," his voice echoed up into the far reaches of the cavern, "is my realm. A realm not of Fire. Not of Earth. A realm that encompasses both and is neither. Fire is the hammer." He raised a fist into the air and it seemed to Talisman that flame flickered through his veins. "Earth is the anvil." He held out a hand. "Together we have forged something new." He brought his fist down upon his palm. The ground seemed to tremble and shake, light and shadow danced across the stone walls.

"And you." Order of the Serpent bent down over Talisman, his voice now quiet and intimate. "You have come to take all this away from me. To destroy it." Talisman looked up into black, merciless eyes. "For that, surely, we must put you to death." He turned to the nonthralls who pressed eagerly around him. "The pit!" he cried. "Drive him into the pit. Tear him to pieces with your whips."

Talisman raised his staff over his head, clutched it with both hands. The nonthralls laughed. "Death," they chanted. "Death to the spy." Talisman brought the staff down over a rock, shattering it. A thin spill of water issued from the rock, ran down into a crevice in the earth. There was sudden quiet.

"Fool!" Order of the Serpent spat. The damp earth glistened wetly. There was a faint hissing sound. A cloud of steam drifted up into the air. The spell held an instant longer. The domain was Water. The laws.

"Fool! Damn you!" Order of the Serpent took a step forward. A tremor passed through the earth, faded. "There's a harmony. A balance. You can't simply throw things together and expect—"

A second tremor seized the ground. The shock wave rolled through the cavern, began to build. Dirt and dust drifted down from above, stone ledges fractured. Order of the Serpent was flung to the ground. The nonthralls backed up, looking puzzled and alarmed.

A sudden current of air ripped through the cavern, generating a shrill whistling noise. A nonthrall caught by the current was flung into the pit of tar. A great blast of icy wind followed. Blue bolts of electricity skittered through the air. A waterspout formed over the tar pit, began funneling great steaming gouts of tar into the air currents darting about. Men fled in terror and died. A tremendous pounding reverberated through the cavern. At its crescendo the tortured earth heaved upward, split with a great rending crash. Molten magma erupted from out of the shattered earth.

Talisman was surrounded by the maelstrom, buffeted by the conflicting forces. Tar burned into his flesh, rocks beat down on him. Destruction reigned all about him, the object, and end, of his mission. A pall of blackness descended over Talisman.

The domain was Death. The laws. ∎

© DONALD W. SCHANK

The Authentic Article
by Diane de Avalle-Arce

Brunilla von Eulenspiegel woke up with "Happy Birthday to You" running through her head, played on a xylophone. Fifty and time for another lift. The future wasn't what it used to be, was it? But she wasn't what she used to be either, so they were even. More or less.

"Sa-am!" she squalled, finding only her mane of tawny hair on the other side of the bed, fanned out like kelp in shallow water. Never you mind what she used to be. The question was, what's today's role? Brunilla liked to get into it from word go. "SAM!"

No answer but seagulls squawking and the lazy Pacific lapping the stilts under the LaLa Boatel. The room, quivering with hazy water-reflections, was retro-deco'd like a Miama motel of the last century, even to plastic flamingos holding up the vanity mirror.

"Damned android sense of humor," Brunilla grumbled, but she palmed a wardrobe-knob and pulled out glossy-black Pocahontas-braids, a gaudy plasticotton skirt and seventeen bottles. Snapping her fingers for light, she applied black films to her irises, black bristles to her lids and brows, a Satsuma plum-red dye to her mouth, and finished off the whole thing with a terra-cotta flesh spray.

Swallowing the last of the not-coffee, she spun the skirt around her ribs just under the breast line, hung a quarter-pounder emerald between cantilevered mammary constructs, and slipped a pair of golden cuff-bracelets with tails and fangs on each forearm.

On cue the door swung open and Sam appeared. "Happy Birthday," he said, bowing over her hand like Clark Gable in the ballroom scene in *Gone with the Wind.* Two inches taller, tanned two shades darker than Brunilla, strikingly handsome and practically human, the 14-37-68 series—oh, never mind. *You* know.

"Go to hell," said Brunilla. "Who's the sucker *du jour,* and what've we got for him?"

"'Client,' Brunilla, dear," Sam corrected in a pained tone. "When nothing else

is the genuine article, the professional manner must be perfect. You look marvellous—Senora Feliciana del Rosario de Chagras, you will be persuaded to sell the precious heritage of your remote *estancia* of Yucatan to the Prince of Tineiblas."

Flipping the bed into the wall, he pushed a table in front of the window. Sun poured through plastic oleanders onto the clay figurines he set out one by one: a bowl on crocodile feet, dregs of dried bloodstains in the bottom; a cross-legged skeleton playing a bone flute; a pair of waltzing scorpions; a dog with a human head carrying a small person in its mouth. The details were exquisite, primitive objects from another time, a bluer sea and a brighter sun.

Brunilla assumed a brooding, Mayan look. She spoke slowly, with a marked accent. "I onnerstan'—nice patina on thees, what ees it?"

"Pyrites, calcium sulphite, some other stuff. The bloodstains are my new formula. Like it?"

"Looks just like certified plasticopies at the Archeological Exhibit," said Brunilla without the accent. "If the client wants to pay a hundred times the official price, he *is* a sucker."

"Nonsense, dear. Would you deprive him of the illusion of finding something illegal, unique, imperfect, *authentic*? Of course he could have anything he wants, roboformed of ultimaplastic. That's why he doesn't want it. Human psychology."

"Which isn't your weakness, Sam."

"I don't," he said judiciously, "deny there are some differences between the technically-human like yourself and us of human technology. But since the United Stockholder's Act of 2032 I am legally a person and—wish you a happy birthday."

"Why, Sam, that's the nicest thing you've said in a long—"

"Time. I hear the lift coming up." Moving smoothly to the door, like the servomech he originally was, Sam opened it as Brunilla resumed her pre-Columbian aspect.

Hoisting the heavy-duty lashes over a smoldering glare, she was startled. The prince was huge—he towered. For a moment the massive figure wavered like a water-image, a trick of the light, no doubt, or a momentary clouding of Brunilla's dark lenses, as was the impression of vast shadowy wings behind the big shoulders. He entered, with a slight, distinguished limp.

"Your 'Ighness ess mos' *bienvenido*," said Brunilla, recovering like the old trouper she was and turning the sultry up to max. "Onlee to your 'Ighness I bring myself to sell heirlooms *de mi casa*, ancient pricelss artifacts—"

"Plastic is plastic," said the prince with a Middle European accent thicker than soup. Bowing in an off-hand manner, he plucked the emerald off Brunilla's sternum with one huge hairy hand. "The stone is rather good, though, a cut above the ones they make in New New Jersey."

"Your 'Ighness is pleased to joke," gasped Brunilla, holding onto her accent with difficulty. "Thees stone is real, jus' like the figures of my ancestors."

"Just like," agreed the prince. "My compliments to your forger. The manipulation of beryllium and aluminum allotropes is an art. But REAL? You've never known the meaning of the word." He made a commanding gesture, including Sam. "Now I will take the liberty of showing you experienced 'dealers' the genuine article."

From under the flowing folds of his jacket, the Prince of Tinieblas produced a crystal big as his fist, yellow as amber, cold as ice, burning with unearthly fire like a frozen star.

"Now this," he said, holding it up in front of the con artists, "is authentic, the oldest and rarest object you can imagine."

"Ooooh!" Brunilla breathed. "I've never seen anything so lovely—it's getting bigger."

The great jewel expanded, pulsing with purple and orange and green flashes, beating like a heart as the prince held it above Sam's outstretched hand.

"What is it? Merely the irreducible core of the killer comet which destroyed most of the biosphere of this planet roughly forty million years ago," stated the prince.

Brunilla yearned for the wonderful golden jewel, swallowing sunlight like a hundred years' worth of photosynthesis at once, focus of all rich and splendid and amazing things ever; but she wrinkled her nose. Under the scent of ozone and kelp from the open window, the all-pervasive acetone smell of ultimaplastic and her own pre-Columbian perfume, there was a whiff of something she couldn't quite put a name to.

She shot a look at Sam. His classic features were as dispassionate as the charioteer of Delphi. But Brunilla, with the advantage of long association, heard a hoarse desperate note, like a drowning man calling for help, as he snapped, "Never heard of it. Provenance of the item?"

"Oh, if you must be pedantic," said the prince, letting the crystal spin on his palm, bigger and more dazzling every minute. "I believe the earliest documentary reference is to be found in the Egyptian Book of the Dead. But you may take it on the best authority—mine—that it was revered in Atlantis before that continent sank. The whereabouts of the crystal were unknown until the explosion of Krakatoa in 1883, your time. We find it next in Japan 1945. Presence verified in Berkeley before California parted company with the continent in—"

"Cut the puffery," said Brunilla, although she was unable to take her eyes from the gem whose own baleful light paled the sunshine. "What would we want with it? And who are *you*? You seem to know our business is faking antiques, but what's *yours*?"

The prince giggled, an eerie high sound like breaking glass. "Oh, I'm a real prince, you can count on that. As for the jewel, make up your minds quickly. The object is in effect a solar storage battery, and it is dangerous to let it absorb too much energy."

He set it down on a chair. Already the light seemed to heat their blood to boiling, sinking into their marrow, from the glorious and unique object. What was the paraphernalia of the sacrifice of a mere 10,000 victims to the nemesis of a million species?

Brunilla knew Sam was frantic with desire as was she, but the strange smell was stronger, and there was something—fishy?—about it.

"I might be interested," said Sam, with an affectation of coolness that fooled none of the three. "I was looking for some trinket for Brunilla's birthday. How much?"

"Ah!" said the prince. "A birthday present? Most suitable. I'm a sentimental creature at heart! I'll let you have it for a—purely nominal sum."

"What's nominal?" Sam snapped back with automatic suspicion, while his eyes followed the madly pulsating jewel in the royal paw.

"Why, your names!" tittered the prince, holding the other hand over his mouth. "Only your names!" Quick as the flick of a snake's tongue he whipped out a stiff paper wrapped around an antique pen with a long nib. "Sign right here on the dotted line—ah, this pen appears to be dry. Your pardon." With a quick powerful movement he jabbed the penpoint into the heel of Sam's hand.

Brunilla snatched at the paper. "Sam, aren't you going to read this first? It says *'per nomina et anima mei'*. What's that all about?"

"Merely a formality, dear lady. a legal expression you needn't worry your head about, like 'In God We Trust' on coins, you know!" He chuckled richly as Sam scrawled his signature across the document in rusty red. "Now here's *yours*, my dear!" Looming over her, pointed pen in hand, he grabbed for her wrist. The fingers closed on the fake gold armlet.

Brunilla snatched her arm out of it and retreated, her eyes showing white rings around the dark lenses like a panicky horse.

"SA-AM!" she yelped. "I don't like this deal!"

On his face was an expression she'd never seen, and he licked his lips; his eyes were fixed on the huge jewel filling the room with unbearable yellow light and a choking smell of sulphur matches. Then the prince rushed at her. Brunilla whipped her full skirt to one side, like caping a bull, as she leaped for the window.

Scattering potted oleanders, she

cleared the rail and dived down, down, down, into the cloudy blue Pacific, swollen with a thousand melted glaciers and warm as dishwater. She sank beneath sunny top layers, down through darker, murky fathoms, and touched bottom where spiny lobsters waved jointed feelers and stirred the pebbles in the mud. Safe, for the moment, from the baleful gem and the menacing prince.

A bitter thought came, why not stay there? Weighted by her paraphernalia, she could ease her bursting chest and stretch out on the silty sea floor. Let crabs gnaw her bones clean and baby octopuses play pick-up-sticks with them. Sam could go to hell with his own friends in his own way.

But the air in her lungs tugged her up, and she thought maybe she'd like to see the hazy sky one last time, green as composite turquoise in fake squash-blossom earrings. She pulled off her heavy skirt and jewelry and rose. The contact lenses floated off her eyes and drifted away like tiny molluscs, but she couldn't see much anyway because oxygen starvation darkened her sight and roared in her ears.

Instead she looked inward and backward, a long time ago when there was a little girl named Mary Lou Kazowka who wanted a Robobarbie doll more than anything, before a big girl who called herself a lot of names waited for the Big Break in New Hollywood. Then weepies came in on the plug-in head-screens, and she took up with Sam, way back when androids had to be accompanied by a human person at all times—yes, it had been a long time. And Sam was funny and kind and could always think of something to do whate-

ver happened. Until now.

Something swelled and burst, deep inside Brunilla, where cosmetic lasersurgery didn't reach, and grew faster even than the deadly diamond. When her head broke the surface, she took a few deep breaths, and swam for the service-port of the LaLa Boatel.

THE PALM-lock was dubious about her cold salty hand, but opened. The light and heat were intolerable, like a furnace. The diamond was bigger than a basketball now, corruscating, pulsing like a live angry thing. Dripping and tangled, less dressed than even contemporary modes approved, Brunilla stepped into the huge cold shadow cast by the *ci-devant* Prince of Tinieblas.

He turned like a buffalo about to charge, with Sam folded up like a package in the crook of his arm. He hissed.

"None of that, now," said Brunilla in the voice she used for deadbeat clients. "The contract is void. Not worth a tin half-yen piece."

"Yess?" said the prince, unpleasantly. "I think you will find it iss quite in order. Your confederate sssigned away his sssoul, no delivery date specified. Sssso—"

"Just you wait a minute. Sam is an android. Legal status as a person, blood to sign with and all the rest, but the Stockholders' Act of 2052 doesn't say zip about a soul. So legally he has no such thing, and your contract isn't worth the parchment it's written on." Brunilla panted like the spin cycle of a heavy-duty washing machine, but she stuck to her point.

His Infernal Highness clutched the curled body tighter. Sam moaned. "Well!

That's arguable. But possession is the other nine points iss it not? Still, I am nothing if not magnanimous. If *you* sign a contract, I'll make it payable on natural demise, and give back the android meanwhile. Fair enough?"

Brunilla, dripping on the carpet, shading her true-blue eyes against the hellish jewel shooting out lasers of colored light, said, "Not quite. I'm too old for birthdays. Take back the diamond and give me Sam's contract and I'll sign. But——" as the prince, grinning like a coal scuttle, flourished his pen, "I'll do the inking myself."

She turned her back and slapped the contract down on the table, sweeping away the clutter of pre-Columbian artifacts. Sucking her finger, she waved the parchment back and forth to dry a rusty-red 'Brunilla von Eulenspiegal' across the bottom. "All right?"

"Jusst fine. Until we meet again!" said the prince, smiling nastily. He punted Sam into her arms, and (Brunilla didn't quite see how it happened) cupped the sun-swollen crystal in his hands and vanished with it.

Brunilla fainted, heavily and full-length. Perhaps due to inner-ear disturbance from her dive, she seemed to hear "*Arivaderci!*" echo in the suddenly darkened room.

SHE CAME to with Sam shaking her and saying, "Brunilla, is that you? Is that you?"

"Who else?" she muttered. But the face in the mirror was an Egyptian mummy most unkindly disinterred. No wonder he couldn't recognize her: it was beyond robosurgery. A couple of big fat real tears leaked into the wrinkles as she surveyed the damage the comet-heart had done.

That wasn't all. It turned out Sam was stone-blind from staring at the crystal, Nemesis or whatever it really was; his forger's hands were as clever as ever but he could no longer fake the lustre of an antique patina.

So they had nothing but each other, and that's how Blind Sam and the Lady in the Mask got started. They traded the last of their stock for a second-hand electronic zither, and sang in the lounge to pay off their bill at the LaLa Boatel.

You know their signature ballad, 'Diamond Eyes'—a synthesizer could never quite duplicate that husky voice, hauntingly just off-key, or the drop-dead zither in the background. Melt the heart of a customs inspector. *You* know. The genuine article.

But you still wonder if she had to pay up on her bargain with the prince. Who knows? She was almost as much plastic and silicon as Sam was—must outweigh any soul she had to start with. But it's doubtful she lost more than her looks, because she not only signed 'Brunilla von Eulenspiegel' instead of 'Mary Lou Kazowka,' she used Sam's special formula fake pre-Columbian blood. ∎

Thrill

by Will Greenway

Crystal walked down the shadowy street feeling cold stares. She'd left her Chesterwood high-rise to get a rush by walking through bagtown. Flash a little gold and some spotless duralon and the scags came to call. She took risks to break the tedium of her corporate life. She also did it to make her bodyguard, Gerron, angry. Maybe this time he'd drop his shields and she'd see the man under the armor.

It gave her a sense of power to be able to draw Gerron here against his wishes. He insisted on keeping his anonymity. She retaliated by forcing him to jump through hoops. He'd threatened several times to let Crystal suffer her folly rather than keep indulging her taste for danger. Each time, he'd show up and get her out of trouble. She was too valuable.

She walked faster, glancing around to see where Gerron was. She saw nothing but darkened streetsides, barred windows, and smog-stained brickwork. The air smelled metallic; the caustic remnants of the mortigene toxins. The sanitation crews used them to clean up the biohazards found here in New Angeles' ghettos.

Crystal forced down concern at not seeing Gerron nearby. Using the holo-empathic abilities of his armor he could go invisible. He did it to discourage her. She couldn't be sure if he'd carried out his threat. So far he'd never failed to put his armored body between her and the vermin. Fists, knives, bullets, photon blasts —all met the same resilient wall.

She tucked her dark hair into the collar of her jacket and glanced back. Something big moved in the shadows. She kept walking, feeling her heart pick up tempo. Alive—not dead like her bio-stricken father, not vegetized like her chip-popping brother.

Cats yowled in an alley. Down the street, turboelectric vehicles hummed across an intersection.

Crystal glanced around for some evidence of Gerron. Sometimes she could find him by looking for inconsistencies where fog or dust blew around his camouflaged form. Ground mists eddied near a light pole across the street. A glint in the shadows.

That's probably him.

A broad figure clad in rags walked down the sidewalk behind her. A big man, enough to make three of her. Something metallic in his hand caught the light from a street lamp.

A gun.

She steeled herself. Gerron could handle it. To see him in action, to be in the fight; that was part of what made her take chances. It made him mad and forced him to talk to her. After years of being her guard, she'd heard his real voice only last month.

The scene sprang like a *tri-vid* in her mind. They had stood on a rooftop looking across the color-spangled city. The chill breeze carried the alkali scent of sanitizing agent, remnants from the cloud seeding the night before. Crystal's gold bodysuit felt damp and looked transparent in places from the exertion of running. Panting, she leaned against the rail. She'd tried to outrun Gerron up ten flights of stairs and failed to increase the margin between them by more than a meter.

She felt his gaze. Crystal turned and stared at the smooth mirror sheen of his face plate. She imagined seeing narrowed green eyes staring out at her. The contours of the blue durathene carapace suggested a muscular physique, a futuristic knight in shining armor.

She'd always fantasized what he looked like underneath. She'd never been able to coax him into removing his helmet. Even threatening to fire him didn't work. He remained simply another of the enigmas she inherited when her father died.

His voice came through an electronic filter, hollow and alien. "I'm here to protect you, yet you try to make my job difficult. Big-G knows there's enough scags who'd pay top creds to have you snuffed. Don't make it easy for them."

She stepped up to him, fingers running down the cool material. "All this money means zip if I can't feel free. I *need* a thrill once in a while. Otherwise I'm as dead as father."

He snorted and took her hand. Even sheathed in heavy gauntlets his touch was delicate. "You mean, you'll *end up* as dead as your father."

She frowned. "You worry too much."

Gerron folded his arms. Servo motors hummed in the armor. She longed to see the look of consternation on his face. An electronic click, the hollow voice replaced by an exasperated baritone. "Drek. You don't worry enough. Push it, missy, and we'll lose you. Then the *govs* will seize the corp."

Crystal took a step back. Never having heard his real voice before, it startled her. It didn't sound raspy or dark, nor did it roll out the way a singer's voice might. Nothing in the accent gave any clues about the face behind the mask.

That irritated her. "So what if the *govs* get it? If I die, no big wiz. No one cares anyway." She turned away and stared at the horizon. In the distance, lasers cast a dazzling filigree across the clouds.

Gerron stepped closer and his tone dropped. "Crystal, you have to consider more than yourself. Many people will suffer if the *govs* take over."

It made her heart ache. Father wasting away in a hospital bed. Put there from stressing over her chip-popping brother who cranked himself into a life support module on BTL chips. Such a waste, both of them. She'd been left to manage the legacy of this cred guzzling corporation, balancing books, handling the board and performing negotiations. It sucked the life from her until she felt like a shell, bitter and empty.

"I've already spent too much time catering to people who don't give a wiz about me. I'm honoring dad's last request and keeping this scag corp afloat. So don't tell me how to live."

He sighed. "Not how to live. How to stay alive."

Crystal looked back. For a moment she thought she saw green eyes through the face plate. "Gerron, it simply doesn't matter."

He gripped her shoulder. "It matters to *me*."

A CAN clattered on the sidewalk behind her. The figure walked quickly now. Gerron usually stopped them long before they got this close.

Something's wrong.

Crystal's heart pounded. She ran. The figure broke into a sprint.

One of her high-heels caught in a crack. She stumbled against a sooty wall next to a gap between two buildings. Before she could move again a huge hand engulfed her shoulder.

A hard object shoved into the small of her back.

"Make like ice, moms."

She froze.

"Turn around."

Crystal stared at the revolver aimed at her stomach. Why didn't Gerron intervene? The hulk used the gun to push her back. The sound of her heels echoed as she backed into the alley. Heart thundering, she retreated, scattering dust, roaches, and old refuse. Her back struck a wall. No place to run.

Why was Gerron waiting? Was he trying to scare her? She felt perspiration matting her dark hair. Nails digging into the crumbling brick, she stared at the square of light framing the alley exit.

Seeing this drug-riddled zombie, she stopped thinking of him as a man. It stared with eyes dilated to the point no color remained. Pawing at her zipper, its fingers left gray streaks on the fabric.

"Gerron!" Squirming she scanned frantically for the telltale shimmer that would mark his reappearance. She listened for the reassuring buzz of his holo field dropping. She heard nothing.

The man snarled and slapped a grimy hand across her mouth. It felt rigid and cold. A foul taste made her recoil.

He spoke in a husky voice. "Close your port, missy." A ring of metal pressed against her cheek. His lips pulled back in a grin.

Crystal shuddered. Had something happened to Gerron? Her stomach felt leaden. She'd die in an alley a victim of her own foolishness. Nothing would remain but a corporate estate claimed by the *govs* and a ten line obituary in the daily data-script.

She forced herself to remain still. An ache between her eyes grew with each heartbeat.

It grunted, face close to hers. "Nice meat, stay still and I might let you jam."

She averted her face and steeled herself as he ran his hand down her arm. Crystal wished she could shut off her nerves and quell the growing panic. If she freaked this drek-head would geek her.

She looked for anything that would help. Broken bottles, crushed lactate cartons and breakfast boxes lay scattered around several overstuffed biolene sacks crammed into the skeletal remains of some freight boxes.

Nothing useful as a weapon. My only chance is if he's so jacked, I can get around the corner before he shoots.

He fumbled at the zipper of her jacket.

The thought of this *thing* touching her bare flesh sent electricity sizzling through her. She prayed to big-G that this drugger could still feel and rammed a knee into his groin.

A groan. She smacked his wrist sending the gun flying into the refuse. A shove sent him crashing to the dirt.

Crystal plunged for the exit. A hand snagged her ankle. She threw out an arm as the ground rushed up at her. A crunching sound. Fire shot through her wrist. She rolled onto her haunches and kicked at his head with a spiked heel.

The drugger warded off the next strike. He growled and pinned her legs, then clawed his way up her body.

She twisted and groped for a hand hold. Finding none, she hammered at the exposed portions of his face. It felt like pummeling a side of beef. She struck at him until her hand bled. Snarling, his face came closer. The alley flickered gray and brown. Her breaths came in staccato gasps.

His weight ground her back into the concrete. She swung an elbow, trying to gouge an eye or break bone. He blocked, grabbing her wrist. A vein throbbed in his forehead.

"Not sly, vix. Gonna have to die now."

His weight squashed out all her wind, leaving no air to scream with. Steely fingers gripped her throat. She beat at his arms but they might as well have been rock. Stars danced in her vision.

"Gerron!" The plea died in her throat.

She saw no mercy in his lifeless eyes. This was the penalty for foolishness. The pain in Crystal's arm faded. White halos blossomed around the objects in sight.

The crushing pressure seemed to lessen. Rainbows of color danced across everything. Bells crashed with diminishing volume. A dreamy detachment overtook her. The pounding of her heart slowed.

Gerron. Why had he failed? Was this an act of spite?

She took the chances simply to get Gerron's attention. To hear his angry voice had been more pleasing than the wiz-brained banality she faced every day. At least Gerron cared.

The alley spun, the last dregs of her life vanishing down a filthy drain. The leering visage loomed over her.

He obviously was drawing out the ordeal to make her suffer.

So tired. Why had she fought so hard? In a way the drugger was doing her a favor by bringing an end to the indifference and misery.

"Come on you scag-worm," she croaked. "Do it." Tears distorted everything. Her lungs hurt. "Nothing matters anymore. Get it over!"

Crystal grabbed his throat. The movement sent jangles of pain through her bad wrist. His felt clammy and rigid.

He only stared at her as she squeezed with all her strength. The grip on her throat loosened. She heard a familiar crackle and the drugger melted into a robotic form. A mirrored visor rolled back and green eyes stared at her. "It matters to me. This enough of a thrill for you?" ■